Samuel French Acting Edition

Harrigan 'n Hart

Book by
Michael Stewart

Music by
Max Showalter

Lyrics by
Peter Walker

Songs of the Period by
Edward Harrigan & Dave Braham

Production Consultation by
Nedda Harrigan

Based on *The Merry Partners* by
Logan E.J. Kahn

SAMUELFRENCH.COM   SAMUELFRENCH.CO.UK

FOR PRODUCTION ENQUIRIES

UNITED STATES AND CANADA
Info@SamuelFrench.com
1-866-598-8449

UNITED KINGDOM AND EUROPE
Plays@SamuelFrench.co.uk
020-7255-4302

Each title is subject to availability from Samuel French, depending upon
country of performance. Please be aware that *HARRIGAN 'N HART* may
not be licensed by Samuel French in your territory. Professional and
amateur producers should contact the nearest Samuel French office or
licensing partner to verify availability.

Stock licensing fees are quoted upon application to Samuel French.

No one shall make any changes in this title(s) for the purpose of production. No part of this book may be reproduced, stored in a retrieval system, or transmitted in any form, by any means, now known or yet to be invented, including mechanical, electronic, photocopying, recording, videotaping, or otherwise, without the prior written permission of the publisher. No one shall upload this title(s), or part of this title(s), to any social media websites.

For all enquiries regarding motion picture, television, and other media rights, please contact Samuel French.

MUSIC USE NOTE

Licensees are solely responsible for obtaining formal written permission from copyright owners to use copyrighted music in the performance of this play and are strongly cautioned to do so. If no such permission is obtained by the licensee, then the licensee must use only original music that the licensee owns and controls. Licensees are solely responsible and liable for all music clearances and shall indemnify the copyright owners of the play(s) and their licensing agent, Samuel French, against any costs, expenses, losses and liabilities arising from the use of music by licensees. Please contact the appropriate music licensing authority in your territory for the rights to any incidental music.

IMPORTANT BILLING AND CREDIT REQUIREMENTS

If you have obtained performance rights to this title, please refer to your licensing agreement for important billing and credit requirements.

LONGACRE THEATRE

S) A Shubert Organization Theatre

Gerald Schoenfeld, *Chairman*   Bernard B. Jacobs, *President*

Elliot Martin, Arnold Bernhard and
The Shubert Organization

present

A New Musical

Book by Michael Stewart

Music by Max Showalter   Lyrics by Peter Walker

Songs of the period by Edward Harrigan and David Braham

Based on material compiled by Nedda Harrigan Logan and

The Merry Partners by E. J. Kahn, Jr.

starring

Mark Hamill
Harry Groener

Christine Ebersole
Amelia McQueen

featuring

Tudi Roche

Kenston Ames Cleve Asbury Clent Bowers Mark Fotopoulos
Michael Gorman Roxie Lucas Merilee Magnuson Alison Mann
Amelia Marshall Barbara Moroz Christopher Wells Oliver Woodall

Scenic Design by	Costume Design by	Lighting Design by
David Mitchell	Ann Hould-Ward	Richard Nelson

Music Supervision Orchestrations & Arrangements by	Musical Director	Sound Design by
John McKinney	Peter Howard	Otts Munderloh

Hair Design by	Casting	Production Stage Manager
Masarone	Warren Pincus Marjorie Martin	Mary Porter Hall

Choreographed by

D. J. Giagni

Entire Production Directed by

Joe Layton

Originally Produced by the Goodspeed Opera House
Michael P. Price, Executive Director

**The Producers and Theatre Management are Members
of The League of New York Theatres and Producers, Inc.**

CAST

(in order of speaking)

Stetson	MARK FOTOPOULOS
Edward Harrigan	HARRY GROENER
Tony Hart	MARK HAMILL
Archie White	CLENT BOWERS
Old Colonel	CLEVE ASBURY
The Colonel's Wife	BARBARA MOROZ
Eleanor	ROXIE LUCAS
Andrew LeCouvrier	MARK FOTOPOULOS
Martin Hanley	OLIVER WOODALL
Sam Nichols	CLENT BOWERS
Alfred J. Dugan	CHRISTOPHER WELLS
Felix Barker	CLENT BOWERS
Judge	MARK FOTOPOULOS
Annie Braham Harrigan	TUDI ROCHE
Johnny Wild	MARK FOTOPOULOS
Billy Gross	CLEVE ASBURY
Chester Fox	KENSTON AMES
Lily Fay	MERILEE MAGNUSON
Elsie Fay	BARBARA MOROZ
Ada Lewis	ROXIE LUCAS
Mrs. Annie Yeamons	ARMELIA McQUEEN
Jennie Yeamons	AMELIA MARSHALL
Harry Mack	CHRISTOPHER WELLS
Photographer	KENSTON AMES
Judge Hilton	CHRISTOPHER WELLS
Nat Goodwin	CLEVE ASBURY
Captain	MARK FOTOPOULOS
Newsboy	KENSTON AMES
Newsgirl	AMELIA MARSHALL
Belle	BARBARA MOROZ
Gerta Granville	CHRISTINE EBERSOLE
Adelaide Harrigan	MERILEE MAGNUSON
Uncle Albert	CLENT BOWERS
Newspaperman	KENSTON AMES
William Gill	MARK FOTOPOULOS
Doctor	CHRISTOPHER WELLS
Nurse	MERILEE MAGNUSON

STANDBYS UNDERSTUDIES

Standbys understudies never substitute for listed players unless a specific
announcement for the appearance is made at the time of the performance.

Edward Harrigan and Tony Hart—Christopher Wells; Gerta Granville—Merilee Magnuson;
Annie Braham Harrigan—Barbara Moroz; Mrs. Annie Yeamons—Roxie Lucas;
Martin Hanley, Archie White, Felix Barker, Sam Nichols, Uncle Albert—Michael Gorman.

Swings: Michael Gorman, Alison Mann.

MUSICAL NUMBERS

ACT ONE

Scene 1. Stetson's American Music Hall, Galesburg, Illinois, 1871.

"Put Me in My Little Bed" .... Tony Hart
"Wonderful Me" .... Harrigan and Hart

Scene 2. New York City.

Scene 3. The Theatre Comique.

"Mulligan Guard" .... Harrigan and Hart

Scene 4. U.S. Courthouse, Worcester, Mass.

"Put Me in My Little Bed" .... Tony Hart

Scene 5. The Theatre Comique.

"I Love To Follow a Band" . . Edward Harrigan and Company
"Such an Education Has My Mary Ann" .... Harrigan, Hart, Company
"Maggie Murphy's Home" . Annie Braham, Edward Harrigan, Sam Nichols, Company
"McNally's Row Of Flats" ..... Mrs. Yeamons and Company
"Something New, Something Different" ..... Harrigan, Hart, Company

Scene 6. The Theatre Comique.

"That's My Partner" .... Harrigan and Hart

Scene 7. Outside the New Theatre Comique, Opening Night.

Scene 8. Old Nieuw Amsterdam.

"She's Our Gretel" .... Harrigan, Hart, Mrs. Yeamons, Company

Scene 9. A Restaurant, Later that Evening.

"What You Need Is a Woman" .... Gerta Granville

Scene 10. The New Theatre Comique.

"Knights of the Mystic Star" ... Mrs. Yeamons and Company
"Girl of the Mystic Star" .... Gerta Granville and Men
"Mulligan Guard" .... Harrigan and Hart

ACT TWO

Scene 1. New York City and the Park Theatre.

"Skidmore Fancy Ball" .... Sam Nichols, Harry Mack, Johnny Wild, Billy Gross
"Sweetest Love" .... Ada Lewis, Elsie Fay
"The Old Barn Floor" .... Johnny Wild, Jennie Yeamons, Chester Fox, Lily Fay

"Silly Boy" . . . . Gerta Granville, Billy Gross, Harry Mack
"Mulligan Guard" . . . . Harrigan, Hart, Company
"We'll Be There" . . . . Harrigan, Hart, Company
SCENE 2. Harrigan's Tour, 1880 to 1886.
"Ada with the Golden Hair" . . Annie Harrigan, Johnny Wild,
Billy Gross
"That Old Featherbed" . . . . Harry Mack, Fay Sisters
"Sam Johnson's Colored Cakewalk" . . . . Sam Nichols,
Jennie Yeamons
"Dip Me in the Golden Sea" . . . . Harrigan, Mrs. Yeamons,
Company
"That's My Partner" . . . . Edward Harrigan
SCENE 3. Backstage, Wallack's Theatre.
"I've Come Home To Stay" . . . . Tony Hart
"If I Could Trust Me" . . . . Tony Hart
SCENE 4. New York City.
"Maggie Murphy's Home" . . . . Martin Hanley, Lily Fay,
Mrs. Yeamons, Ada Lewis
"I've Come Home To Stay" . . . . Hart and Girls
SCENE 5. New York Hospital.
"I Need This One Chance" . . . . Gerta Granville
SCENE 6. The Park Theatre. March 22, 1888.
"I Love To Follow a Band" . . . Annie Harrigan and Company
"Mulligan Guard" . . . . Harrigan, Hart, Mrs. Yeamons
"Something New, Something Different" . . . . . Harrigan, Hart,
Company

TIME: 1871 to 1888

7

AUTHOR'S NOTE

Harrigan 'n Hart was an enormous success when it premiered at Michael Price's theatre in Chester, Connecticut. It lasted only a few performances when it transferred to Broadway early the next year. I cannot with any certainty give you a valid reason for its failure—perhaps it was blown up to unreasonable proportions—but it was not well received. Yet in preparing this printed version I was struck by the fact that the show was not only good, but also funny, exciting, and moving, and—although I'm a bit hesitant to say the word—important.

Musical comedy has been this country's most innovative contribution to world theatre. We invented it, we perfected it, and we still do it best. And no other play or musical that I know of explores the beginnings of this uniquely American art form better than the one you now have before you. For despite what myths have been circulated, musical comedy as we know it today began with Edward Harrigan and Tony Hart at the Theatre Comique on lower Broadway in the latter half of the last century. And a kaleidoscopic look at those beginnings is what *Harrigan 'n Hart* offers.

The show is fast paced as was the country at the time. It charges along with the excitement of a period in American history when there was nowhere to go but up. It abounds in the broad humor and vigorous music of that unique epoch. All the excitement that the words "musical comedy" connote is embodied in the story of those two extraordinary men, and I am convinced that anybody who feels about musicals as I do will share my enthusiasm. Okay, I'm partial, I am the author, but read it and I think you'll see what I mean.

Some thoughts I'd like to pass on if you do the show. Mount it modestly as indicated. A cast of fifteen is maximum. With the exception of three or four key characters, everybody should double. The original cast list (page 5) indicates the doubles we chose; you might have other ideas. There should only be one set: a theatre of the period with the proscenium remaining always visible and other locales indicated as simply as possible. Same goes for costumes. In Chester we used a basic costume for everybody with additions of a hat, a jacket, an apron, a bow, etc., as the script requires. The current orchestrations are for nine pieces. You can do it with five. Or even piano and percussion in a pinch. Decor, costumes, etc., should never get in the way of the energy and pace of the piece.

As you can see, I care very deeply about *Harrigan 'n Hart* and I hope that you will be intrigued enough to produce it. If you do, I would appreciate your letting me know through Samuel French so that if I am in the area I might see your production. You might be more successful with it than we were.

Thank you,
Michael Stewart

EDWARD HARRIGAN (1845–1911) was born and raised in New York. He abandoned his seaman's career in San Francisco for the stage, as a "sketch artist," and worked his way east through the mining towns. In time he was not only an actor, but director, producer and author of countless sketches, 33 plays and over 200 songs. It was William Dean Howells who first called Harrigan "the Dickens of America," due to his realistic writing of New York life and people, plus his creating a new native dorm of drama—telling a full story with music, rather than variety sketches with olio.

From 1871 to 1885 he and Tony Hart were the beloved *Harrigan and Hart* team, first as variety, and then with Harrigan's expanded plays, and surrounded by their warm and talented company. Their best known works were the "Mulligan Guards" series, satiric but affectionate stories and characters of the New York melting pot.

After the two men unhappily parted, Harrigan kept his company intact, and in 1890 he built his own Harrigan's Theatre (later to become the Garrick Theatre and then the first home of The Theatre Guild) on West 35th Street in New York. Ill health forced him to retire in 1903, and he died in 1911. But in 1908 his protege, George M. Cohan, brought tears to his eyes with the song Cohan wrote as a tribute to his idol . . . "H-A-double R-I-G-A-N spells Harrigan!"

TONY HART (1855–1891) was born Anthony Cannon in Worcester, Massachusetts. His lively pranks sent him to reform school, from which he soon fled for the variety and minstrel stage, where he met and teamed up with Ned Harrigan in 1871. Hart was referred to as "joy and sunshine," and had a compelling magnetism in both men's and women's roles. *The Boston Traveler* said "Hart could play all the parts that seven Harrigans could write, and Harrigan could write what seven Harts could play." Tony Hart married the actress Gerta Granville, which started the friction leading to the break-up of *Harrigan and Hart* in 1885. After that he performed in few plays, disappointingly, and then, suffering from paresis, died in an insane asylum, tragically only 36.

—Program notes by Ann Connolly, granddaughter of Edward Harrigan

Harrigan 'n Hart

ACT ONE

[MUSIC NO. 1: OVERTURE]

SCENE 1

Near end of OVERTURE we segue to sound of small pit band as CURTAIN rises on Stetson's American Music Hall, *Galesburg, Illinois in the year 1871. Set encompasses onstage and backstage areas of theatre with only specific being an olio which announces name of theatre and lists among the acts,* "Edward Harrigan and His Colleens, Irish Songs & Dances," *and somewhat further down,* "Master Anthony Hart! Assisted by Archie White."
CURTAIN has come up on a tableau of backstage activity with HARRIGAN and the COLLEENS frozen in the middle of an onstage jig step C. *As OVERTURE comes to a climax, scene comes to life with STETSON, the manager of the theatre, looking at his watch as he paces angrily back and forth and STAGEHANDS watch HARRIGAN and the GIRLS as they go into climax of their number.*

STETSON. (*as turntable turns right and HARRIGAN and COLLEENS finish dance and take bows*) Damn little punk, who does he think he is? (*to STAGEHAND*) Wally, get the Lilybelles on, they're closing the show!

WALLY. Ain't that kid goin' on next?

STETSON. That 'kid' don't happen to be here so do as you're told! (*As WALLY starts getting LILYBELLES together, HARRIGAN starts off.*) Damn little punk!

HARRIGAN. What's the matter, Mr. Stetson?

STETSON. That kid's late again, and I told him twice already I want my acts backstage at least a half-hour before show time! This may be Galesburg, Illinois and not New York, New York, but I have standards I expect you people to. . . .

HARRIGAN. Take it easy, Mr. Stetson, he's probably on his way down from the dressing room, anyhow Archie White opens up the act.

11

STETSON. (*indicating a MAN dozing in a chair*) Not tonight he don't! Been oiled since the matinee. Can't even stand up! Actors, bottom of the barrel, the lot of you. (*to STAGEHANDS who pass with bed*) Put that back, the Lilybelles are closing the show!

HARRIGAN. (*trying to get ARCHIE up on his feet as FIGURE IN OVERCOAT starts down center*) Wait a minute, Mr. Stetson, let me talk to him. Come on, Archie, on your feet, you can do it, come on boy. . . .

FIGURE IN OVERCOAT. Hi, Stetson, how's the house?

STETSON. Huh? (*seeing who it is*) Why you fresh punk! How dare you come in here almost one hour late? This may be Galesburg, Illinois, and not New York, New York, but. . . .

TONY HART. (*for that is who it is*) What're you getting so excited about, Al, I'm all ready! (*taking off his coat, revealing himself in little girl's nightdress*) Master Anthony Hart at your service.

STETSON. Oh you're ready, are ya? As ready as your partner is I hope, because he's good and ready—And don't call me Al!

TONY HART. (*as WHITE tries to get to his feet*) Is that what the fuss is about? A couple of drinks between shows? Look, compared to how he usually plays the act it's like he took the pledge. (*To WALLY*) Get the girls off, Wally, we're going on!

HARRIGAN. (*as WALLY signals to LILYBELLES*) White can't even stand, kid. Look, I've watched the act all week, if you want some help I can. . . .

TONY HART. Who says he has to stand, I'm the star, I do the moving. But thanks anyhow, uh. . . .

HARRIGAN. Harrigan.

TONY HART. Right. Listen, you're not bad, Hannigan, I been watchin' you too, material's old hat but I got some ideas. (*to STETSON as LILYBELLES take hasty bow, HARRIGAN shakes his head in amusement*) By the way, Al, I want to talk to you about my salary, twenty-five a week ain't much for an act chokes 'em up the way we do, I thought maybe a little increase, for instance. . . .

STETSON. An increase! Fresh punk, one comes in late, the other drunk, then nervy enough to ask me for a. . . .

TONY HART. We'll talk terms later, Stetson, I'm on.

[MUSIC NO. 2: PUT ME IN MY LITTLE BED]

(*And he starts onstage as we come up on* child's bedroom, *bed* R., *unseen man on ladder tossing handfuls of snow which appear to fall outside window* U.S. *ARCHIE WHITE seated back to audience in chair* L. *as TONY HART, now a golden-haired twelve year old little girl, looks lovingly at him and sings.)*

TONY HART.
DADDY DEAR, DADDY DEAR
IT IS GROWING LATE I FEAR
AND NOW THAT MOMMY'S LIVING UP IN HEAVEN OH
  SO BLUE
THERE'S NO ONE IN THIS LONELY HOUSE
BUT YOU
TO . . .
(as he subtly pushes back ARCHIE's head which has slipped to his chest)
PUT ME IN MY LITTLE BED
PILLOWS ROUND MY LITTLE HEAD
TUCK ME NEATH MY COVERS WHILE YOU STROKE MY
  HAIR
SING ME TOORA-LOORA AS I SAY THIS PRAY'R . . .
(ARCHIE is sliding slowly but surely out of chair, TONY gently kicks him back.)
GOD BLESS MOMMY!
GOD BLESS DADDY!
GOD BLESS ME AND BABY FRED . . .

(ARCHIE, bottle in hand, leans out and sings "BLESS FRED!" TONY puts his arm back as he climbs into his lap.)

TONY HART. *(continued, as ARCHIE tilts dangerously left)*
NOW MY BEDTIME'S GROWING NEAR
SO PICK ME UP, MY DADDY DEAR
AND PUT ME IN MY LITTLE . . .
(Under his breath, still smiling) Watch it! *(singing again)*
BED.

(MUSIC continues as WHITE gets to his feet and starts off past the bed into the wings. He is pushed back, passes bed again as TONY hangs onto bedpost, then crashes into drop, and finally causes man on ladder throwing snow to crash to ground as TONY reaches desperately through window for something to hold on to. As ladder crashes we hear cry of "Kill the lights". LIGHTS go off for a second then come on again as DADDY and TONY come back on.)

DADDY. (*his back to audience*) Now go on, sweetheart, you were saying?

TONY HART. (*realizing that it is no longer ARCHIE*)
GOD BLESS MOMMY!
GOD BLESS DADDY!
GOD BLESS ME AND BABY FRED

DADDY. (*turning around so we see it is HARRIGAN*)
BLESS FRED!

TONY HART. (*as HARRIGAN takes him to bed, tucks him in*)
NOW MY BEDTIME'S GROWING NEAR
SO PICK ME UP, MY DADDY DEAR
AND PUT ME IN MY LITTLE . . .
(*as LIGHTS iris down*) Goodnight, Mommy! (*and out*)
BED!

[MUSIC NO. 2A: LITTLE BED BOWS]

(*LIGHTS up for bows. TONY forces HARRIGAN to take one with him, then they both come off as STETSON starts angrily on.*)

STETSON. So all he had to do was sit, hah? You're the star!

TONY HART. I did it, didn't I?

STETSON. No thanks to your bum partner, you can finish the week, Hart, then out.

TONY HART. (*Stepping out of nightdress, he is fully dressed underneath.*) Why wait till Saturday? Call tonight's show the finish, no charge, a benefit—listen, the way you're running this dump you're gonna need one. (*as STETSON gasps, to HARRIGAN*) Not bad, kid. You covered me a little on the finish but not bad. Wait till I get my coat and I'll show you what you did wrong, uh. . . .

HARRIGAN. Booth. Edwin.

TONY HART. Yeah, well nice goin' Eddie. (*to STETSON*) See you around, Al. (*And he's gone.*)

STETSON. Why, you little. . . .

HARRIGAN. Take it easy, Mr. Stetson, he's a kid.

STETSON. I don't care! Benefits for me, hah? Well, I'll take care of Mr. Anthony Hart in a way he may not like so much. Let me tell you a few things you might not know about that kid! Underneath those curls you know what he is? Nothing but a little. . . . A little. . . .

STAGEHAND. (*passing*) Punk.

STETSON. Yeah. (*as he exits*) What are you waiting for, strike that set, you girls get outa them costumes, this ain't no social club. . . .

TONY HART. (*coming back with suitcase, cap*) All right, let's go!

HARRIGAN. Go?

TONY HART. There's a bean wagon over on State Street, we can get something to eat and talk about the act.

HARRIGAN. Mine?

TONY HART. Ours!

HARRIGAN. Sorry, I've already got an act, with the Colleens.

TONY HART. You mean *had*. Doorman told me they're quittin' end of the week to go off on their own.

HARRIGAN. So I get two others. I've managed pretty well so far.

TONY HART. No, you haven't. You're twenty-six, been touring eight years either bottom of the bill or after the acrobats, first with Ed Rickey playing mostly mining camps then a couple of seasons as advance man for Mme. Rentz' Female Minstrels— kinda liked that, didn't you—now the Colleens are leaving and you can't hire two others because they took the costumes with them!

HARRIGAN. The doorman?

TONY HART. The doorman.

HARRIGAN. All right, it's all pretty accurate except for what he doesn't know—that I've written a new act. A single.

TONY HART. Won't work. You need someone to bounce things off! Like me.

HARRIGAN. Not so sure about that, I've heard some things about you too.

TONY HART. I know, fresh, unreliable, pushy, swell-headed, loud-mouthed and a punk—Well let's get one thing straight right now! It's all true. (*HARRIGAN laughs, the kid's brashness appeals to him.*) Well, whadda ya say?

HARRIGAN. But you already have a partner.

·TONY HART. Archie White? Left ten minutes ago with two suitcases and a bottle. I'm available.

[MUSIC NO. 4: WONDERFUL ME]

HARRIGAN. (*as MUSIC comes up*) I could use someone I guess. The managers do want teams. And I want to try my luck in New York—I've got some ideas about a new way to do shows that I can't do on my own! All right, what can you do?

TONY HART. You saw me last night, didn't you?

HARRIGAN. What else?

TONY HART. Everything! (*And he sings.*)

NAME IT, I'LL DO IT
DUTCH, IRISH, JEW,
IT DOESN'T MAKE A DIFF'RENCE WHO IT MIGHT BE
CAUSE AFTER ALL IS SAID AND DONE
YOU'LL FIND THAT EV'RY SINGLE WONDERFUL ONE
  OF THEM'S
WONDERFUL ME!

ASK ME, I'LL PLAY IT
SHOUT, WHISPER, BRAY IT
POSITIVELY JUST THE WAY IT SHOULD BE
FROM FULLA GLOOM TO FULLA FUN
YOU'LL FIND THAT EV'RY SINGLE WONDERFUL ONE
  OF THEM'S
WONDERFUL ME!

COME LET ME TAKE YOU TO THE COUNTRY OF YOUR
  CHOICE
WITH NOTHING BUT MY HANDS AND FEET
AND SWEET, SWEET VOICE

THEN I WILL SING IT
STRUT, BUCK AND WING IT
TILL I MAKE IT EV'RYTHING IT CAN BE
AND SURE AS MORNIN' FINDS THE SUN
YOU'LL FIND THAT EV'RY SINGLE WONDERFUL ONE
  OF THEM'S
WONDERFUL ME!

HARRIGAN. Irish!

TONY HART. (*instantly becoming same*)

IN THE KITCHEN ARE POTATOES FOR THE CHILDREN
  AND THE HOGS
WHERE THE FAM'LY FALLS ASLEEP BY COUNTIN'
  PUDDLES ON THE BOGS
AND WE ARE ALWAYS CARTIN' COW-DUNG IN TO
  PLUG THE LEAKY LOGS
I'M A HUNDRED AND ONE PERCENT HIBERNIAN!

HARRIGAN. Dutch!

TONY HART. (*another change*)

IN DA VINDMILL VERE I VOULDN'T VORK IF I VAS
  VELL-TO-DO
I KEEP GETTING SPLINTERS FIRST IN VON, UNDT
  DEN DE UDDA SHOE
GOTT IN HIMMEL UNDT MEIN FINGERS IN DA DYKE
  IS TURNING BLUE
YA, I AM A HUNDRED UNDT VON PERCENT DUTCH!

HARRIGAN. Italian!

TONY HART. (*a third instant switch*)

COME SE DICE MY GOLDEN-A VOICE-A IS MUSIC-A
  TO-A MY EAR
WHENEVER I SING-A DA VERDI, ROSSINI HIMSELF-A
  STAND UP-A AND CHEER
BUT IN-A RIGOLETTO, I FELL ON-A MY STILETTO
AND-A HOW YOU SAY, CUT OFF-A MY CAREER
IO SONO CENTO UNO PERCENTE ITALIANO!

(*as MUSIC continues*) Well, what do you think of me? Never
mind I know—tremendous—now how's this for a title for the
act—Master Anthony Hart and Company! (*HARRIGAN just
smiles.*) Master Anthony and friend? (*HARRIGAN nods no.*)
Tony Hart assisted by Edward Harrigan! (*Still nothing; TONY
gives up.*) Harrigan and Hart? (*HARRIGAN puts out his hand,
they shake, and sing.*)

HARRIGAN & HART.

THEN WE CAN SING IT
STRUT, BUCK AND WING IT
TILL WE MAKE IT EV'RYTHING IT CAN BE
KIDS AND WIDOWS
BUMS AND MONKS
UNHOLY SAINTS
AND HOLY DRUNKS
ALIVE OR DEAD IT'S LIKE WE SAID YOU'LL SEE

(*Sound of train coming in as HARRIGAN grabs his suitcase.*)

YOU'LL FIND THAT EV'RY SINGLE WONDERFUL ONE
  OF THEM'S

TONY HART.

EV'RY SINGLE ONE OF THEM'S
WONDERFUL,

HARRIGAN.

WONDERFUL,

HARRIGAN & HART.
WONDERFUL, WONDERFUL,

(*TONY dashes back, grabs his suitcase, hops on the turn-table with HARRIGAN and sings.*)

TONY HART.
ME!

[MUSIC NO. 4A: WONDERFUL ME PLAYOFF]

(*And we segue directly to . . .*)

SCENE 2

New York City *in the 1870's. TONY and NED on a street in front of the Comique Theatre.*

HARRIGAN. . . . It's all set! Dave Braham's going to run over the music with the orchestra at four, I've sent Sam Nichols his lines and he'll be there right after his matinee, and here's the best part, Tony—a four week contract if we go over!

TONY HART. Ned, are you sure about this, this is New York, they've never even heard of us. . . .

HARRIGAN. They will after tonight! Look around you, Tony. Did you ever see such a city? The best and worst from every part of the world dumped here by the thousand every day—fighting, loving, drinking, marching—we put that on the stage and they'll eat it up!

TONY HART. And they won't mind seeing themselves? Chinks and colored and micks and Jews?

HARRIGAN. They'll love it! That crowd's as much a part of New York as all those elegant ladies singing of Spring and canary birds up at Tony Pastor's! We'll give them *themselves*, Tony!

TONY HART. I still wish it wasn't at the Comique. It's the toughest house in town. They don't throw things from that gallery—they jump right down and get you!

HARRIGAN. Master Anthony scared? I don't believe it!

TONY HART. Are you crazy, what've I got to be scared about, it's a fella like you worries me, I'd never forgive myself if they harmed you, you know how fragile and sensitive you are. (*as they start off*) Look, if they start anything you get offstage and I'll go into "Put Me In My Little Bed", they wouldn't dare murder a twelve year old little girl, anyhow not one carrying a couple of bricks, you just get off, Ned, and. . . .

(*But by now they're gone as we come up on.* . . .)

SCENE 3

The Theatre Comique *on lower Broadway. The most awful noise, shrieks, shouts, whistles, fights, the bellow of candy butchers selling their wares, as the PLAYERS in a dramatic sketch try to make themselves heard.*

USHER. (*over general bustle*) You heard me, out!

KID. Whadda ya mean, I paid my money!

USHER. Then where's ya ticket?

KID. Somebody swiped it!

USHER. (*beginning to eject KID*) No ticket, no seat, out!

KID. Help, somebody help, he's throwin' me out, ya know why, because I'm a orphan wid no one to protect me, that's right a orphan, if you don't believe me ask my Mudder, she's upstairs in the balcony, Ma, he's throwin' me out. . . .

VARIOUS PATRONS. (*through above*) Yeah, 'trow 'im out! Ah the poor kid, he's an orphan! Shut up all of yiz, I'm tryin' to hear the actors! I just heard 'em, tell the kid to make more noise! Candy, getcha fresh candy, over here while it's fresh, candy, fresh candy, etc., etc.

OLD COLONEL. (*finally making himself heard*) But where is she? Where is my daughter Eleanor?

VOICES. Yeah, where is she? Where's Elly?

HIS WIFE. (*overriding them*) She is upstairs, Edward, putting on the last ball gown we had made for her before the war made fine silks and satins impossible to obtain.

OLD COLONEL. Her ball gown! That can mean only one thing! That cloud of dust I noticed on the Memphis road signifies the imminent arrival of. . . .

HIS WIFE. Captain Andrew LeCouvrier! He swore he'd return for her birthday and that cloud might very well be. . . .

VOICES. Her lover! Him! Andy!

HIS WIFE. (*batting away an apple core thrown from audience with her fan*) Correct. But hush, she comes! (*arms outstretched*) My daughter!

OLD COLONEL. (*as 'star' comes on*) Eleanor! Congratulations on your sixteenth birthday!

(*That brings down the house. Whistles, cries of "Sixteen!", applause. ELEANOR acknowledges applause, ignores the rest.*)

ELEANOR. Did I hear somebody call my name?

VOICE. 'Twas me, girlie, you fiancy, I'm up here waitin' fer ya!

OLD COLONEL. That cloud of dust on the Memphis road, Eleanor, we fear it might be Andrew.

ELEANOR. It is Andrew, I would know that particular cloud of dust anywhere. And he brings with him the tattered remnants of his regiment.

HIS WIFE. Then they will all be killed! There are Union soldiers everywhere!

VOICE. Ooh, there's one! Right behind the door!

ELEANOR. Yes, he will be killed, but what is one life more or less if this dreadful war will at last be terminated. (*A military drum is heard offstage.*)

OLD COLONEL. Look, daughter, a body of men is marching up the road to the house!

HIS WIFE. But wait, a Union detachment commanded by Major O'Brien has also seen them!

VOICE. Down with the Irish! Kill the micks!

ELEANOR. Back, all of you! Andrew must see me alone!

(*In snappy close-order drill, ANDRE LE COUVRIER and his MEN march on. At end of drill ANDREW steps forward.*)

ANDREW. Eleanor!

ELEANOR. (*as if seeing him for first time*) Yes?

ANDREW. I have returned — As promised. (*A shot cracks out — a hair late, but what matter. He falls.*)

ELEANOR. (*Stepping forward, her hoop skirt covering ANDREW LE COUVRIER's head. He quietly tries to push it back to give himself breathing space through following.*) [MUSIC NO. 4B: CIVIL WAR U.S.] My lover is gone. I shall marry no more. This

war has claimed its last sacrifice for even this morning comes
news that peace has been declared at Appomattox Courthouse.

VOICE. She coulda' said something before.

ELEANOR. (*as MUSIC comes up*) Yes, the Union is saved but
at what price? Mamma, take my ball gown and rend it to tatters!
Pappa, boys of my late fiance's regiment, and Union soldiers. I
shall dance. . . . (*head down*) No more!

(*CURTAIN swishes down. Applause, jeers, items thrown onstage. Company takes many bows, last one by ELEANOR
alone as man starts on down right.*)

[MUSIC NO. 4C: CIVIL WAR BOWS]

MARTIN HANLEY. (*manager of the Comique*) Sam, what are
you doing here?

SAM NICHOLS. (*dressed in oversized version of OLD COLO-
NEL's costume*) A little favor for Ned Harrigan. Excuse me,
Martin.

HANLEY. But she's still taking her bows!

SAM NICHOLS. Ned said now. See you later, Martin. (*crossing
to ELEANOR, Dutch comic accent*) Hey, liebchen, dere's an-
odda cloud of dust on de road, listen, how many luffers you ex-
pecting?

ELEANOR. (*backing away from him*) I beg your pardon!

SAM NICHOLS. Not dot way, my little schnitzel! Dot's vere de
cloud of dust is coming from!

[MUSIC NO. 5: MULLIGAN GUARD]

(*And true to his word, a huge cloud of dust rolls on. ELEANOR
chokes and coughs as she retreats and HARRIGAN and
HART march onto stage. They are dressed in sorry imita-
tions of previous military costumes, jackets too big, breeches
too tight, etc. TONY carries drum, NED two rifles. For a
moment ELEANOR is tangled up with them, then TONY
gives her drum and pushes her off. NED hands him rifle and
they go into parody of close order drill we have just seen,
hitting each other with guns [which occasionally go off],
stepping on each other's feet, marching into each other, all
the old burlesque and vaudeville bits. They finally get into
step as vamp begins and they step forward and sing.*)

HARRIGAN & HART.
WE CRAVE YOUR CONDESCENSION
TO TELL YOU WHAT WE KNOW
OF MARCHING IN THE MULLIGAN GUARD
FROM BAXTER STREET BELOW
OUR CAPTAIN'S NAME WAS HUSSEY
A TIPPERARY MAN
HE CARRIED HIS SWORD LIKE A RUSSIAN DUKE
WHENEVER HE TOOK COMMAND

WE SHOULDERED ARMS
AND MARCHED AND MARCHED AWAY
FROM BAXTER STREET
WE MARCHED TO AVENUE A
WITH DRUMS AND FIFES
HOW SWEETLY THEY DID PLAY
AS WE MARCHED, MARCHED, MARCHED
IN THE MULLIGAN GUARD!

(*A Dance, eccentric in style, but with a sense of total unity so
that it will seem there are not two actors onstage, but one
Harrigan 'n Hart. End with a spectacular step or two as
they sing.*)

HARRIGAN & HART.
WHEN THE BAND PLAYED GARRY OWEN
OR THE CONNAMARA PET
WITH A RUB DUB DUB, WE'D MARCH IN THE MUD
TO A MILITARY STEP
WITH THE GREEN ABOVE THE RED, BOYS
TO SHOW WHERE WE COME FROM
OUR GUNS WE'D LIFT WITH A RIGHT SHOULDER
   SHIFT
AS WE MARCHED TO THE BEAT OF THE DRUM

WE SHOULDERED ARMS
AND MARCHED AND MARCHED AWAY
FROM BAXTER STREET
WE MARCHED TO AVENUE A
WITH DRUMS AND FIFES
HOW SWEETLY THEY DID PLAY
AS WE MARCHED, MARCHED, MARCHED
IN THE MULLIGAN . . .
MARCHED, MARCHED, MARCHED

IN THE MULLIGAN . . .
MARCHED, MARCHED, MARCHED
IN THE MULLIGAN GUARD!

[MUSIC NO. 5A: MULLIGAN GUARD BOWS]

(*And the house comes down. Applause, cheers, TONY and NED run breathlessly off after the bows. There should be a disconnected quality about this next brief scene, perhaps a light change, something that frames it, sets it apart, a suspended moment.*)

HARRIGAN. Do you hear that? They like us!
TONY HART. Why shouldn't they? We're wonderful!
HARRIGAN. And this is only the beginning, Tony! We'll get a company, build a theatre, write plays with music to sing to, march to, dance to, music all over 'em!
TONY HART. And it'll always be us, won't it Neddy?
HARRIGAN. (*taking his hand*) Always be us!

HANLEY. (*Bursting onto scene, LIGHTS return to normal.*) Harrigan! Hart! What are you waiting for? Do more!
HARRIGAN. We haven't got anything more.
HANLEY. Then do that again!
TONY HART. The same thing?
HANLEY. That's what they want! Get out there in front of the curtain before they tear the house apart! Go on!

[MUSIC NO. 5B: MULLIGAN GUARD OFFSTAGE]

(*He pushes them back on. We hear cheers, then muffled MUSIC as they sing to audience off right. HANLEY listens from backstage.*)

MAN. (*who has been watching last of this*) They're pretty good.
HANLEY. They're better than that, my friend. (*looking at him*) Who are you?
MAN. No one you know, Mr. Hanley.
HANLEY. Then what the hell are you doing back here? No one's allowed backstage during a performance. (*He calls.*) Charlie!
MAN. I'm allowed, Mr. Hanley. (*takes out card*) Official business for the state of Massachusetts.

HANLEY. (*ignoring card*) What are you talking about? I've never even been to Massachusetts. Look, Mr. . . .

MAN. Dugan. Alfred J. And it's not you we're interested in. It's Mr. Anthony Hart. (*A burst of applause, cheers, heard through curtain.*) You see, he got no right to be here.

HANLEY. Who says he don't! He got a contract with me for four weeks!

DUGAN. And he got one with us too. For another twelve months. At the Worcester, Mass. Detention Home. That's right, Mr. Hanley—Detention Home. You see, Master Anthony left us without notice and that's not nice.

HANLEY. A prison?

DUGAN. We don't like to say that word, Mr. Hanley. Anyway, he's got another year due us—Plus whatever time the Judge hangs on him for leaving so sudden. (*HARRIGAN and TONY HART, both exhilarated, have come off during last of this. Through following they stop and listen.*) But that'll all be decided July 28th at the U.S. Courthouse in Worcester, unless you or somebody else wants to go his bail. (*to TONY HART*) Great show, kid, you'll have to do it again for the gang at Worcester. Now how soon do you think you can get out of that outfit?

HARRIGAN. Wait a minute! What is this? Who is he?

HANLEY. A cop, Ned. Or something like that.

DUGAN. With a court order to take Master Anthony back to his native state. You see, they miss him.

HARRIGAN. Tony. . .

TONY HART. It's true, Ned. I ran away from the Home about four months before we met up. I didn't think they'd bother with me as long as I kept out of the state.

DUGAN. Oh we don't ordinarily. But when someone makes a special request that we look into a case. . . .

TONY HART. Stetson! (*in answer to HARRIGAN's puzzled look*) "This may be Galesburg, Illinois and not New York, New York. . . ."

DUGAN. Stetson it is. Always were a bright little chap, weren't you? Now come along, sonny, it's getting late.

HARRIGAN. Get your hands off him!

DUGAN. Look, friend, in case you don't know I happen to be an officer of the law.

HARRIGAN. I don't care who you are, get your hands off him!

HANLEY. Wait a minute, both of you! (*The scuffle stops.*) Look, Mr. Dugan, a few minutes ago you mentioned the word bail. Now if it isn't too unreasonable, maybe I can put it up. Why don't you come into my office.

DUGAN. That's more like it. (*straightening his clothes*) Use force and I use force. (*going with MARTIN HANLEY*) Be reasonable. . . . And I can be reasonable too.

(*And they exit* L. *LIGHTS start down through following as TONY HART, whistling casually, crosses right to* Dressing Room Area, *begins removing tie, etc.*)

HARRIGAN. (*after a moment*) Tony, why?

[MUSIC NO. 5C: TRUST ME UNDERSCORE]

TONY HART. Why what, Ned?

HARRIGAN. Why were you in that place?

TONY HART. No reason.

HARRIGAN. There must be some reason, Tony.

TONY HART. Oh I guess there was. But no one in particular. My folks had me put in.

HARRIGAN. How could your own folks have you. . . .

TONY HART. I made a lot of trouble. Kid trouble I guess, but my old man said it had to be nipped in the bud so he put me in the Home. Oh, they changed their minds about a month later but it was too late, I wouldn't go back with them. Putting me there was their idea and I made them stick to it. I don't turn back, Ned. No matter what it does to me. I don't turn back.

HARRIGAN. (*suddenly*) I'm going up there with you. (*MUSIC out.*)

TONY HART. To Worchester?

HARRIGAN. To talk to that Judge.

TONY HART. Forget it, Ned, I'll take care of him.

HARRIGAN. Tony, he's probably a Federal Judge and you don't 'take care' of a Federal Judge. You'll need a lawyer— Felix Barker—he's used to working with actors!

TONY HART. What's a lawyer going to say except they're in the right? I can handle him my own way but I'll need some help from you and a couple of the boys.

HARRIGAN. (*starting off* R.) No, Tony, this time we're doing it according to the rules, we get Felix Barker and go up there and. . . .

TONY HART. (*exiting after him*) All right, but just in case I'll bring along a couple of the guys, Louie, and Red, and Big Charlie, and. . . .

(JUDGE's Bench *has started on through this as we come up on . . .*)

Scene 4

U.S. Courthouse, Worcester, Mass. *JUDGE rapping for attention.*

Judge. . . . Mr. Barker, would you please explain to Mr. Harrigan that this is a court of law and that extraneous speeches by friends of the client, even though well intentioned, are not in order!

Harrigan. I know that, Your Honor, but I've listened to you quote laws and cases all day and it seems to me you've missed the point! The boy was put into the Home to make him a useful citizen and since he is that now, why send him back? I'm sure the Worcester Detention Home is a splendid institution and the stories of excessive cruelty, whipping, total lack of sanitary and health facilities are—even though thoroughly documented—greatly exaggerated. But the boy no longer belongs there!

Judge. I appreciate that fact, Mr. Harrigan, but this is strictly a matter of law! The boy must first be returned to the Home and then and only then can legal measure to effect his release be instituted, therefore with all due respect to Mr. Barker and yourself I must order that. . . .

[MUSIC NO. 6: LITTLE BED/JUDGE SCENE]

(*At that moment a voice is heard in the courtroom.*)

Tony Hart. (*starting on in wig and nightgown followed by five or six musicians playing in dinner clothes*)
PUT ME IN MY LITTLE BED . . .

Judge. What's this?

Tony Hart. (*As TWO STAGEHANDS with bed and MAN with ladder, snow, and bucket, bring up the rear.*)
PILLOWS ROUND MY LITTLE HEAD . . .

Judge. I'm warning you, this is a court of law! (*TONY and musicians group themselves around the bench.*)

TONY HART.
TUCK ME 'NEATH MY COVERS WHILE YOU STROKE
MY HAIR . . .
(*MAN gets on ladder and begins tossing snow on the JUDGE.*)
JUDGE. I'll have you cited for contempt! And singing in
Massachusetts without a permit!
TONY HART.
SING ME TOORA-LOORA AS I SAY THIS PRAY'R . . .
JUDGE. (*as TONY starts climbing up to him*) Please, there are
reporters, this might get into the papers . . .
TONY HART. (*Right up there beside him, full voice, as MAN
throws snow.*)
GOD BLESS MOMMY!
GOD BLESS DADDY!
GOD BLESS . . .
(*picking up name plate*)
HIS HONOR JUDGE FRANCIS B. HOLLINGSHEAD

(*TONY signals to HARRIGAN and FELIX BARKER.*)

JUDGE. Now they know my name, what will I do?
HARRIGAN & FELIX BARKER.
NOW HIS BEDTIME'S GROWING NEAR
SO PICK HIM UP, YOUR HONOR DEAR . . .
JUDGE. (*giving up*) All right, I'll do it. Anything to get him
out of here!
HARRIGAN & FELIX BARKER. (*as JUDGE does so*)
AND PUT HIM IN HIS LITTLE . . .
JUDGE. (*banging his gavel*) The court remands the defendant
into the custody of Mr. Edward Harrigan! And may God have
mercy on his soul!
ALL. (*including JUDGE*)
BED!

(*TONY sticks his tongue out at HARRIGAN as LIGHTS go
out and immediately up on . . .*)

SCENE 5

SPOTLIGHT D.R. *HARRIGAN talking to someone unseen.*

HARRIGAN. Thanks, kid. Listen, you newsboys are the toughest audience in New York and when you like the show we know we're good! Hey, I want you to meet our company. (*as they come out*) Tony, you know. And that's Dave Braham, our musical director. Annie Braham, his daughter. Sam Nichols, our Dutch comic. And Johnny Wild!

[MUSIC NO. 7: FOLLOW A BAND]

(*A blare of MUSIC as DAVE BRAHAM raises his baton. HARRIGAN, ANNIE BRAHAM, NICHOLS and WILD become a line of* seated *minstrels as Olio comes in and TONY HART sings.*)

TONY HART.
MUSIC CHARMED THE DEACON
A MEMBER OF THE CHURCH
HE'D HEAR A BAND AND WEAKEN
IT CHARMED HIM OFF HIS PERCH
ONE DAY WITH THE COLLECTION
BEHIND THE BAND HE FLED
AND WHEN THEY CAUGHT HIM LATE THAT NIGHT
WHY THIS IS WHAT HE SAID

TARA, TARA TARA, I HEARD THEM CORNETS PLAY
BIM BUM, THEY BEAT THE DRUM, MY FEET BEGAN
  TO SWAY
SOUSA, I DO DECLARE, YOUR MARCHES AM SO
  GRAND
JUST CAN'T HALT, IT AIN'T MY FAULT
I LOVE TO FOLLOW A BAND!
(*As OTHERS,* still seated minstrel fashion, *do oompahs and choreographed movements behind him:*)
SEVEN MORNINGS LATER
AGAIN HE DID THE SAME
HE MADE IT TO DECATUR
BEFORE THE SHERIFF CAME
HE HAD THE PREACHER'S WALLET
HIS WIFE AND ALL HIS GOLD
AND WHEN THEY SAID, WHY THIS WON'T DO!
THIS MOVING TALE HE TOLD
    TONY HART/OTHERS.
TARA, TARA TARA, I HEARD THEM CORNETS PLAY

BIM BUM, THEY BEAT THE DRUM, MY FEET BEGAN TO
   SWAY
SOUSA, I DO DECLARE, YOUR MARCHES AM SO
   GRAND
JUST CAN'T STOP, AWAY I HOP
I LOVE TO FOLLOW A BAND!

[MUSIC NO. 8: MARY ANN]

(*Direct segue for TONY as he says:*)

TONY HART. Thanks, Mr. Goodwin. Listen, when a fellow actor likes the show we know we're good! Hey, I want you to meet
the company. Ned, you know. . . . (*They have changed to
school-children costumes as Olio of Schoolroom and row of
desks comes on.*) And that's Dave Braham and little Annie, and
Sam Nichols, Johnny Wild, and Gross & Fox!

(*TONY HART makes costume change behind QUARTETTE
and becomes a tipsy schoolmistress who sneaks nips from
bottle in her pocket, then vase, then inkwell, as they sing.*)

SAM NICHOLS, JOHNNY WILD, GROSS & FOX.
SHE'S A DARLING!
SHE'S A DAISY!
SHE'S A DUMPLING!
SHE'S A LAMB!
SHE CAN PLAY WITH EASE
THE PIANO KEYS
SUCH AN EDUCATION HAS MY MARY ANN!
   HARRIGAN.
MY MARY ANN'S A TEACHER
IN A GREAT BIG PUBLIC SCHOOL
SHE GETS ONE THOUSAND DOLLARS EV'RY YEAR
SHE HAS CHARGE OF ALL THE CHILDREN
YOU'LL NEVER FIND A FOOL
FOR MARY GIVES THEM ALL A PROPER STEER
FOR SHE'S STUDIED GREEK AND LATIN
REAL FRENCH AND TIMBUCTOO
YES, GERMAN, SPANISH, TURK AND HINDOOSTAN
SWEET PORTUGUESE AND IRISH
AND JERUSALEM HEBREW
SUCH AN EDUCATION HAS MY MARY ANN!

TONY HART. (*as teacher, as MUSIC continues*) Johnny, I want to talk to you about your grammar! Especially your pronouns!

JOHNNY WILD. I can't help it, teacher, me grammar come from Ireland and that's why she don't pronouns so good.

TONY HART. (*whacking him with ruler*) Another fresh answer like that and you'll get double; that's progressive education. All right, Schultz, tell us what you know about the first president.

SAM NICHOLS. Ja, teacher! De vurst president was Livervurst, undt after him I tink Bratvurst.

TONY HART. You forgot one.

SAM NICHOLS. Vot vas dot?

TONY HART. (*whacking him*) *Knock*vurst! Annie, if you have four and I have two, how do you make it equal?

ANNIE. I give you one.

TONY HART. That's right. Neddy, if I have three and you have one, how do you make it equal?

HARRIGAN. You give *me* one!

TONY HART. With pleasure. (*MUSIC out. And he whacks him.*) And that's what school is for, to make 'em healthy, welt-y and wise. Sing! (*MUSIC up.*)

HARRIGAN & OTHERS.
SHE'S A DARLING!
SHE'S A DAISY!
SHE'S A DUMPLING!
SHE'S A LAMB!
YOU SHOULD HEAR HER TONE
ON THE SOUSAPHONE . . .
SUCH AN EDUCATION HAS MY MARY ANN!

[MUSIC NO. 9: MAGGIE MURPHY'S HOME]

(*Direct segue for HARRIGAN as he takes off school costume and says:*)

HARRIGAN. Thanks, Champ. Listen, when the heavyweight champion of the world likes us, we know we're good! Hey, I want you to meet the company. Tony, you know. And that's Dave Braham and little Annie, Sam Nichols, Johnny Wild, Gross & Fox, Martin Hanley, and the Fay Sisters! (*HARRIGAN puts on jacket and straw hat, and starts toward ANNIE.*)

SAM NICHOLS.
EACH WEEK WHEN WORK WAS OVER

NED CASEY FOUND HIS WAY
  ALL.
TO CALL ON MAGGIE MURPHY
THE BELLE OF AVENUE A
SHE LIVED WITH HER DEAR MOTHER
IN TWO ROOMS CLEAN AND NEAT
AND WHEN HE SAID,
  HARRIGAN.
"ARE YOU AT HOME, MY DEAR?"
  ALL.
SHE ANSWERED OH SO SWEET
  ANNIE. (*with OTHERS harmonizing*)
ON SUNDAY NIGHT
'TIS MY DELIGHT
AND PLEASURE DON'T YOU SEE
TO MEET ALL THE GIRLS
AND ALL THE BOYS
WHO WORK DOWNTOWN WITH ME
THERE'S AN ORGAN IN THE PARLOR
TO GIVE THE PLACE A TONE
AND YOU ARE WELCOME EV'RY EVENING
AT MAGGIE
MURPHY'S
HOME.

[MUSIC NO. 10: MCNALLY'S ROW OF FLATS]

TONY HART. Thanks, Mr. Stewart. Listen, when the owner of New York's biggest department store likes our show we know we're good! Now I'd like you to meet the gang. Ned, you know. And that's Dave Braham and little Annie, Sam Nichols, Johnny Wild, Gross & Fox, Martin Hanley, the Fay Sisters, Ada Lewis, and a new addition to our company—the finest dramatic actress ever to be run out of Macon, Georgia—Mrs. Annie Yeamons!

MRS. YEAMONS. I understand Ellen Terry is in the house. Hey, Ellie, get a load of this! (*Olio of Tenement comes in as MRS. YEAMONS sings.*)
IT'S DOWN IN BOTTLE ALLEY
LIVES TIMOTHY McNALLY
A WEALTHY POLITICIAN AND A GENTLEMAN AT
  THAT
THE JOY OF ALL THE LADIES
THE KIDDIES AND THE BABIES

WHO OCCUPY THE BUILDINGS CALLED McNALLY'S
  ROW OF FLATS!

OH IT'S IRELAND AND ITALY
AND AFRICA AND GERMANY
IT'S HEBREW FOLK AND CHINAMEN
AND SEVEN THOUSAND CATS
ALL JUMBLED UP TOGETHER
IN THE SNOW OR RAINY WEATHER
THEY REPRESENT THE TENANTS
IN McNALLY'S ROW OF FLATS!

HEY, McNALLY!
  TENANTS. (*spoken*) Fix the pipes!
  MRS. YEAMONS.
HEY, McNALLY!
  TENANTS. (*spoken*) We want heat!
  MRS. YEAMONS & TENANTS.
HEY, McNALLY, WE AIN'T GONNA PAY THE RENT!
  MRS. YEAMONS.
HEY, McNALLY!
  TENANTS. (*spoken*) Sweep the stairs!
  MRS. YEAMONS.
HEY, McNALLY!
  TENANTS. (*spoken*) Clean the street!
  MRS. YEAMONS & TENANTS.
HEY, McNALLY, IT'S A LOVELY TENEMENT!
  ALL.
IT NEVER WAS EXPECTED
THE RENT WOULD BE COLLECTED
THEY'D TAKE AWAY THE FURNITURE, THE BEDDING,
  AND THE SLATS
MORE SHOUTIN' THAN A RALLY
THE BATTLES IN THE ALLEY
A-THROWIN' OUT THE TENANTS FROM McNALLY'S
  ROW OF FLATS!

OH IT'S IRELAND AND ITALY
AND AFRICA AND GERMANY
IT'S HEBREW FOLK AND CHINAMEN
AND SEVEN THOUSAND CATS
ALL JUMBLED UP TOGETHER
IN THE SNOW OR RAINY WEATHER

THEY REPRESENT THE TENANTS
IN McNALLY'S ROW OF FLATS!

(*A Dance for COMPANY and MRS. YEAMONS building to climax as they shout.*)

FIX THE PIPES!
WE WANT HEAT!
SWEEP THE STAIRS!
CLEAN THE STREET!
(*shouting*)
HEY, McNALLY!!

[MUSIC NO. 10A: MCNALLY'S BOWS]

(*Direct seque to HARRIGAN as Olio of Tenement goes out and he says:*)

HARRIGAN. (*as MUSIC continues*) Thanks, Your Honor, listen when the Mayor of the greatest city in the world likes our show we know we're good! Now I'd like you to meet the company. Tony, you know. And that's Dave Braham, Sam Nichols, Johnny Wild, Gross & Fox, Martin Hanley, the Fay Sisterw, Ada Lewis, Mrs. Yeamons and her daughter Jenny, and Harry Mack! (*MUSIC out.*)

HANLEY. Ned, the Mayor wants to know what happened to little Annie Braham?

HARRIGAN. Haven't you heard, Your Honor? She grew up. (*ANNIE, wearing more womanly ensemble, comes on.*) Mr. Mayor, I'd like you to meet Mrs. Annie Harrigan.

TONY HART. (*having put on scarf of old Irish biddy through above*) Ooh I'm jealous I am, choosin' a mere chit of a girl over a foine mature beauty like I, I'll kill meself I will, I'll eat me own cookin' and starve to death, no I'll fix 'im, I'll get married meself, how about it, Yer Honor?

(*Two banners drop in, one saying,* "Tonight! On These Premises! Skidmore Ball!", *the other saying,* "Tonight! On These Premises! Mulligan Ball!")

HARRIGAN. His Honor's here to see a rehearsal of the new finale, not to find a bride — lovely as ye are, darlin' — Now let's get on with it!

(*Through this, ENTIRE COMPANY carrying Mulligan or Skid-*

more placards and wearing contrasting marching jackets have lined up behind HARRIGAN on one side and MRS. YEAMONS on the other as he continues:) I'm warnin' ya for the last time, Skidmores, upstairs with the lot o' ye! 'Tis the Mulligan Ball tonight on these premises and I'll stand fer no interference!

SAM NICHOLS. Oh no, Mulligan, you gonna *lie down* for it once my fisticuff here arrives in contact with that fine Hibernian chin.

TONY HART. (*as MRS. MULLIGAN*) Did ye hear that, Paddy darlin'? Oh let me at 'im, oh I'll tear 'im in twain pieces I will, oh I'll rip 'im from stem to stern and if that ain't stern enough I'll give him a piece o' me mind in the bargain!

MRS. YEAMONS. A piece of her mind, that ain't no bargain, but she better not give him two pieces or she won't have nothin' left.

HARRIGAN. I'll give ye one more chance, Skidmores, upstairs with the lot of ye and I'll say no more about it!

SAM NICHOLS. No you don't, Mulligan, upstairs is the Oriental Marchin' and Noodle Society and above that the Hebrew Home Guard is holdin' their social and on the top floor they got the First Annual Baxter Street dog, cat, goat, and poultry show!

HARRIGAN. (*pushing up his sleeves*) It looks like there's only one way to settle this!

SAM NICHOLS. With pleasure! (*adopting fighting stance*) Put 'em up, Mulligans!

HARRIGAN. Put 'em up, says who?

MRS. YEAMONS. Put 'em up, says I!

TONY HART. Put 'em up, says you? (*sparring the air*) Why, I'll lacerate ye; why, I'll mince ye into mince pie; why, I'll habeas yer corpus and salt yer battery too. . . .

[MUSIC NO. 11: SOMETHING NEW, SOMETHING DIFFERENT]

HARRIGAN. (*stepping out of character*) Wait a minute, do that again. (*MUSIC starts a very different vamp as scene continues.*) From "Put 'em up, Mulligans!" Only more.

MRS. YEAMONS. You mean louder?

HARRIGAN. I mean more! Something else. (*as he slips from dialogue into the number with just the barest hint of MUSIC to begin with*)

SOMETHING NEW
SOMETHING DIFF'RENT
SOMETHING NEVER DONE BEFORE

SOMETHING UNEXPLORED AND FRESH AS EARLY
   SPRING
LIKE WHEN A NASTY SO-AND-SO
PURSUES A LADY PURE AS SNOW
INSTEAD OF *TELLING* HIM TO GO . . .
SHE'LL SING!

(*TONY HART catches his fire, and turning to JOHNNY WILD
   standing next to him, beats him on chest as he sings.*)

   TONY HART.
YOU, SIR
YOU ARE A CUR, SIR
THAT'S WHAT YOU ARE, SIR
AND ALWAYS WERE, SIR
SO I WILL NOT, SIR
ACCEPT YOUR FUR, SIR
FOR YOU, SIR
YOU ARE A CUR. SIR!
   HARRIGAN. That's it!

(*TONY tears off his Mrs. Mulligan scarf and joins NED as they
sing.*)
   HARRIGAN & HART.
SOMETHING NEW
SOMETHING DIFF'RENT
SOMETHING NEVER EVEN TRIED
SOMETHING LOOKIN' LIKE IT'S DONE AS IF BY
   CHANCE
LIKE WHEN THE HERO GOES TO MEET
HIS LITTLE DARLIN' HONEY SWEET
INSTEAD OF *WALKIN'* DOWN THE STREET . . .
HE'LL DANCE!

(*Short waltz with FOX as suitor, LILY FAY as his sweetheart.*)

   HARRIGAN & HART, MRS. YEAMONS AND ANNIE.
AND IF DANCE WON'T DO
AND SINGIN'S NOT ENOUGH
WE'LL LET THE FELLAS IN THE ORCHESTRA
STRUT THEIR STUFF!

(*ORCHESTRA stands in the pit and blasts out their interlude as*

*ABOVE FOUR indicate them. By now excitement has spread
to COMPANY as they sing.)*

HARRIGAN & HART and COMPANY.
SOMETHING NEW
SOMETHING DIFF'RENT
SOMETHING WAITING IN THE WINGS
SOMETHING SET TO MAKE AN ENTRANCE—TAKE A
 BOW
WHEN WE COME SAILING THROUGH THE DOOR
WITH SOMETHING NEW AND FURTHERMORE
SOMETHING NEVER DONE BEFORE . . .
 HARRIGAN. (*a shout*)
TILL NOW!
(*as MUSIC continues*) Now the whole scene with music, song,
dance, mayhem, anything and everything!

 SAM NICHOLS, HARRIGAN, MRS. YEAMONS, AND TONY HART.
(*singing the first four lines, then joined in groups of five by rest
of COMPANY as the brawl gets louder and more physical*)
PUT 'EM UP, MULLIGAN!
PUT 'EM UP SAYS WHO?
PUT 'EM UP SAYS I!
PUT 'EM UP SAYS YOU?
(*Brawl is interrupted three times by FOX who appears stage
right as all action stops for a split second and he shouts:*)
 FOX. (*after first eight seconds of brawl, sung*)
BE CAREFUL, MULLIGAN, THE WALLS IS SHAKIN'!
(*after next five seconds of brawl, sung*)
WATCH OUT, MULLIGAN, THE STAIRS ARE BEGIN-
 NING TO CRUMBLE!
(*after next five seconds of brawl, sung*)
MULLIGAN, THE CEILING IS COMIN' DOWN!!

(*And with a dissonant crash of orchestra the ceiling above gives
 way and dummies of Chinamen, Hebrews, dogs, goats,
 chickens, furniture, tumble down making one glorious
 pileup on stage. Last crash and EVERYBODY, as one, suddenly lifts up their heads and sing.*)

 ENTIRE COMPANY.
SOMETHING NEW
SOMETHING DIFF'RENT

SOMETHING NEVER DONE BEFORE
SOMETHING UNEXPLORED AND FRESH AS EARLY
  SPRING!
SOMETHING NEW
SOMETHING DIFF'RENT
SOMETHING NEVER EVEN TRIED
SOMETHING LOOKIN' LIKE IT'S DONE AS IF BY
  CHANCE

WE'LL SING!
WE'LL DANCE!

SOMETHING NEW
SOMETHING DIFF'RENT
SOMETHING WAITING IN THE WINGS
SOMETHING SET TO MAKE AN ENTRANCE – TAKE
  A BOW
WHEN WE COME SAILING THROUGH THE DOOR
WITH SOMETHING NEW AND FURTHERMORE
SOMETHING NEVER DONE BEFORE . . .
(*ALL, led by NED and TONY, triumphant*)
TILL NOW!

(*LIGHTS freeze and immediate segue to. . . .*)

SCENE 6

Bare stage of theatre, *bench with back* D.R., *camera of period
set* U.L. *COMPANY has discarded Mulligan/Skidmore
jackets as JUDGE HENRY HILTON gingerly holds model
of the new Theatre Comique and PHOTOGRAPHER pre-
pares to record the historic moment.*

PHOTOGRAPHER. Patience, patience, just a few moments more!
JUDGE HILTON. We've been here an hour already! If I'd known
it would be all this trouble to build a theatre for your company,
Mr. Harrigan. . . . (*to whomever is standing next to him*) By the
way, did you know that the facade of the new theatre will be
made of Philadelphia pressed brick, practically fireproof.
MARTIN HANLEY. And don't forget the inside, eighteen hundred and fifty seats!

HARRIGAN. Orchestra, balcony, and gallery, plus three boxes on each side with private staircases.

JUDGE HILTON. But the most important is the brick pressed, from Philadelphia, and practically fireproof. . . .

PHOTOGRAPHER. (*through last of this, to TONY HART who reads a newspaper to one side*) Mr. Hart.

TONY HART. Huh?

PHOTOGRAPHER. If you could join the group, we're about ready now.

TONY HART. Oh, sure. Sure.

PHOTOGRAPHER. (*as TONY puts down paper, takes his place*) Now everybody, when I say hold, you hold your breath, done you relax, that's right you seated, you standing, and in the center, Mr. Harrigan, Judge Hilton, and Mr. Hart shaking hands. Now remember, nobody breathes when I say — Hold! (*EVERY-BODY instantly freezes full out as turntables begins moving to reveal traditional period group pose and PHOTOGRAPHER slowly counts.*) One, two, three, four, five, six, seven, eight, nine, ten, eleven, twelve, thirteen — Done! (*A collective sigh as they all take a breath.*) That wasn't so bad, was it? Now all we have to do is check the names. (*Reading from list as by "Here!", by lifting hands, by other signals, all are accounted for. As list is greater than cast, we double more than once.*) . . . . From left to right Mr. Harrigan's business manager and first cousin, Mr. Martin Hanley, then Mr. Harrigan's uncles Fred, George, and Albert, and aunts Amy, Irene, and Grace, all members of the office staff. Next Mr. Harrigan's father-in-law Mr. David Braham and the members of his orchestra, Mr. Alphonse Braham, Mr. Henry Braham, Mr. Theodore Braham, and Mr. Edward Regan.

TONY HART. How'd he get in there?

PHOTOGRAPHER. Mr. Braham's brother-in-law, Mr. Hanley's uncle, and Mr. Harrigan's second cousin.

TONY HART. I see.

PHOTOGRAPHER. Next the backstage staff, Mr. Stanley Nelson, Mr. Martin Reilly, Mr. A.P. Bradley, all nephews if I am not mistaken. (*The boys say,* "Uh huh.") Mrs. Harrigan and her assistants Phyllis and Bernadette.

PHYLLIS AND BERNADETTE. Third cousins once removed.

PHOTOGRAPHER. Then Mr. Harrigan himself and on Mr. Hart's side. . . . (*He looks.*) There is Mr. Tony Hart.

TONY HART. I tried to buy a few relatives but Mr. Harrigan cornered the market. (*They laugh, PHOTOGRAPHER starts dismantling his equipment.*)

ANNIE. (*through above*) Come along everybody, supper is at six sharp, you too, Mr. Keller, come along, come along.

JUDGE HILTON. (*as he goes*) I wonder if I told you about the Philadelphia pressed brick, it's very important you know, the brick is pressed, and it comes all the way from Philadelphia. . . . (*By now stage is almost empty.*)

ANNIE. Ned, Tony, come along!

HARRIGAN. In a minute, dear, just some business to discuss.

ANNIE. (*From off as she exits*) Just a minute, Ned, we're having leg of lamb and I don't want it overdone.

(*She is gone. TONY has again picked up his paper. A moment, then NED speaks.*)

HARRIGAN. Tony. . . .

TONY HART. Yes, Ned?

HARRIGAN. Everything all right?

TONY HART. Of course. Why shouldn't it be?

HARRIGAN. All those Harrigans on the payroll. I know there's a lot of them but Annie has a soft heart and there always seems to be a cousin who needs a job and. . . .

TONY HART. (*putting down paper*) Ned, Ned, I was only joking! I like your relatives. Better than mine.

HARRIGAN. But when I looked round the room and saw all those Harrigans and Hanleys and Brahams. . . .

TONY HART. And one poor lonely Hart in the middle you got worried. Ned, that one Hart is better off than all of them! You write plays for him, all those other Harrigans and Brahams build theatres for him, make money for him, and that poor old Hart comes to the theatre every night and collects fifty percent of what they earn. The more Harrigans I've got working for me the better!

HARRIGAN. Do you mean that?

TONY HART. Ned, if I wanted some Harts around I'd get married and supply them by the dozen! I like being one of a kind.

HARRIGAN. (*Irish*) And that ye are, Tony me boy! (*meaning it*) And by all the saints, nobody knows it better'n me. (*as MUSIC comes up through following*) But I still think we have to do something to even things up!

TONY HART. That's easy, adopt me, then I can be a Harrigan like everyone else, or maybe I can be Aunt Grace's long-lost second cousin, that would make me Martin's uncle, Dave's brother, Annie's stepfather, and either your nephew or maternal grandmother, how about both, I could be the nephew on Tuesdays and Granny the rest of the week. . . .

[MUSIC NO. 12: THAT'S MY PARTNER]

HARRIGAN. (*laughing*)
AH, TONY BOY, I'VE GOT ENOUGH TO KEEP ME
　MEM'RY BUSY
WITHOUT COMMITTIN' TO IT EV'RY NAME FROM "A"
　TO LIZZIE
HELL, THE JOB OF JUST PRODUCIN'
ALL THEM NAMES WHEN INTRODUCIN' THEM
WOULD TAKE THE BETTER PART OF A WORKIN' DAY
WHILE ALL I HAVE TO DO
IS TURN MYSELF TO YOU
AND SIMPLY SAY . . .

THAT'S MY PARTNER
MY PAL
MY CHUM
THAT'S THE FELLA
GOOD FORTUNE
KEEPS ON SMILING FROM

HE'S THE REASON
MY STEP
IS LIGHT
HE'S THE MUSIC
I DANCE TO
MORNING, NOON, AND NIGHT

　　HARRIGAN & HART.
HE'S MY BROTHER
MY OTHER SELF
I'LL WALK MY DAILY MILE WITH
SMILE WITH COME WHAT MAY
I'M HONORED TO SAY
HE'LL BE BY MY SIDE
FOR LIFETIMES TO COME
　　TONY HART.
MY PARTNER
　　HARRIGAN.
MY PAL
　　HARRIGAN & HART.
MY CHUM . . .
　　HARRIGAN. (*as MUSIC continues under*) Now come on,

Tony, there'll be the devil to pay if Annie's lamb is overdone.

TONY HART. Make some sort of excuse for me, will you, Ned?

HARRIGAN. Why? The party's for all of us.

TONY HART. Nat's coming by, we're going out to dinner.

HARRIGAN. Tony, it's not for me to say but. . . .

TONY HART. I know, Nat Goodwin's a wild man, he's been married four times, he's out with a different girl every night, it's fine for him but a boy like you. . . .

HARRIGAN. (*recovering his good humor*) Not it at all, all I wanted to say is that going out all night is fine for a boy like you, but an old man like that. . . . (*TONY laughs.*) All right, off with you. But remember, no more than three girls or three bottles of champagne. Apiece!

TONY HART. (*laughing, as they clown together*)
THAT'S MY PARTNER
MY PAL
MY CHUM
THAT'S THE FELLA
GOOD FORTUNE
KEEPS ON SMILING FROM

HARRIGAN.
HE'S THE REASON
MY STEP
IS LIGHT
TONY HART.
HE'S THE MUSIC
I DANCE TO
MORNING, NOON, AND NIGHT

HARRIGAN & HART.
HE'S MY SHARER
MY BEARER OF
GOOD TIDINGS I'LL BE GLAD TO
ADD TO EV'RY DAY
HARRIGAN.
I'M HONORED TO SAY
HE'LL BE BY MY SIDE
FOR LIFETIMES TO COME
TONY HART.
MY PARTNER
HARRIGAN.
MY PAL

HARRIGAN & HART. (*As HARRIGAN puts out his hand, TONY takes it.*)
MY CHUM!

HARRIGAN. Sure you won't change your mind? Bring Nat if you want!

TONY HART. Thanks, Ned. Another time.

HARRIGAN. All right, Tony. (*starts out, stops*) About all those Harrigans, don't you have someone, anyone, who needs a job? Just to have at least one more Hart on the payroll?

TONY HART. How about the undesirable brother of an unreliable great-aunt in Brooklyn?

HARRIGAN. Exactly what we're looking for! They make the best night watchmen.

TONY HART. Then I'll sober up Uncle Albert and send him around. See you tomorrow, Ned.

HARRIGAN. See you tomorrow.

(*And HARRIGAN goes off. A moment, then we hear sound of VOICES offstage as HARRIGAN evidently meets someone on the way out, "Ned!" "Nat, how are you?" "Never better, Neddy, a joy to see you", and NAT GOODWIN comes on.*)

NAT. Well, let's go, kid. Belle's waiting and she's brought — and this is a quote, Tony — the prettiest girl in New York. And dying to meet the great Tony Hart.

TONY HART. Nat. . . .

NAT. Yeah, kid?

TONY HART. About Ned and me, Nat. What do people think?

NAT. What are you talking about?

TONY HART. Because he writes the plays and all, do they think it's all Ned?

NAT. What kind of damn fool question is that? Look at the marquee, kid. Harrigan *and* Hart! Same size, same letters. Anyhow, it doesn't make any difference what they think, you get half the money, don't you? Well, take it and run, kid. Take it and run.

TONY HART. I suppose you're right. (*as they start out*) What's her name, Nat?

NAT. Lola. Lola Leary and Belle tells me she. . . .

(*FADE OUT and up on. . . .*)

Scene 7

Outside New Theatre Comique *on opening night, CROWD swirling about with the voice of JUDGE HILTON heard from time to time as he goes from group to group.*

JUDGE HILTON. From Philadelphia! Pressed! And practically fireproof. . . .

MARTIN HANLEY. (*talking to GUARDS CAPTAIN*) Andy, you promised! Not over a minute for each one.

CAPTAIN. What kind of ovation is that? The whole regiment's here and they want to let the boys know how they feel.

MARTIN HANLEY. (*as they go inside*) The boys appreciate it, Andy, but not more than a minute each. Ned's written a full three-act show this time!

JUDGE HILTON. Brick! Each one hand pressed. . . .

FIRST NEWSBOY. I got the music! I got it from an usher who swiped it off the fiddle player. Who can read?

SECOND NEWSBOY. I can if it's easy words. (*reading from sheet music as they hurry inside*)
THE ICEMAN AND THE BUTCHER, THE BAKER WITH HIS TARTS

[MUSIC NO. 12A: UNDERSCORE]

JUDGE HILTON. Eight thousand of them. . . .

GERTA. (*coming in with NAT GOODWIN*) It's awfully noisy, isn't it?

NAT. You think this is noise, wait till the play begins! (*to BELLE who is lagging behind*) For God's sake, Belle, get a move on!

BELLE. (*as they start in*) Now he yells at me to hurry! Honest, Gerta, men are the limit, I wish there was something else I liked.

JUDGE HILTON. Practically fireproof and they come all the way. . . .

ANNIE HARRIGAN. Now put on your gloves, Adelaide, I don't want your father to be ashamed of you.

ADELAIDE. He doesn't wear gloves.

ANNIE HARRIGAN. (*as they start in*) He's an actor, they're not supposed to be respectable, that's why we have to be twice as.

[MUSIC NO. 13: GRETEL]

JUDGE HILTON. (*hurrying in as MUSIC of OVERTURE begins*) From Philadelphia!

(*By now stage is empty as we come up on. . . .*)

SCENE 8

Old New Amsterdam. *HARRIGAN and TONY HART as proud Dutch parents in front of olio as two wooden-shoed SUITORS wait with flowers and candy.*

TONY HART. (*heavy dutch accent as vamp continues*) Tell me, husband mine, vy is all dese fellas vaitin' in front of de house?

HARRIGAN. For our little Gretel, vifey mine. Dey is vaitin' for her to come back from her chores.

TONY HART. But dey all got blooms undt sveets, Hansie dearest.

HARRIGAN. Of course dey does, my little tulip blossom. Dey vant her hand.

TONY HART. Vell dey von't haf it, de poor girl only has two and she uses dem both!

HARRIGAN. Her hand in marriage, dumpling! Dey vants to take her to de altar.

TONY HART. Take her to be altered? Vot do dey tink she is, a two-piece suit? I von't haf my Gretel shortened, lengthened, or taken in at the cuffs.

HARRIGAN. (*as tab rises revealing Dutch House and four more SUITORS*) Vot can ve do, Katinka, sweetheart? Dey lufs her. (*and he sings*)
DE ICEMAN UNDT DE BUTCHER
DE BAKER MIT HIS TARTS
DE PLUMBER UNDT DE TAILOR
SHE'S BROKEN ALL DERE HEARTS
TONY HART.
BUT HUSBAND, CAN YOU BLAME DEM?
SHE'S DAINTY AS AN ELF
VY, IF I VAS A FELLA
I'D FALL IN LUF MYSELF
HARRIGAN & HART.
SHE'S A DUCK, SHE'S A DOVE
SHE'S DE VUN DE BOYS ALL LOVE
SHE'S A JEWEL, SHE'S A FLOWER, SHE'S A PETAL

SHE'S A GEM, SHE'S A PRIZE
UNDT SO DAINTY FOR HER SIZE
VOT A CUTIE, VOT A BEAUTY, IS OUR GRETEL!
  SIX SUITORS.
SHE'S A ROSE, SHE'S A PEARL
VAS DERE EVER SUCH A GIRL?
SHE'S A JEWEL, SHE'S A FLOWER, SHE'S A PETAL
SHE'S SO FAIR, SHE'S SO SWEET
UNDT SO LIGHT UPON HER FEET
SHE'S A CUTIE, SHE'S A BEAUTY, SHE'S OUR GRETEL!

(*HARRIGAN and TONY HART begin waltz clog which SUIT-
ORS pick up until TONY HART suddenly shouts.*)

TONY HART. Hansie, I see somevon coming from de direction
of de barn!
HARRIGAN. Dot'll be her! I sent her to milk de cow! Over here,
Gretel, sveetheart!
MRS. YEAMONS. (*in Dutch maiden costume, oversized hat,
wooden yoke across her shoulders with two milk pails*) Comink,
Papa! (*MRS. YEAMONS enters, and sings.*)
I'M A DUCK, I'M A DOVE
I'M DE VUN DE BOYS ALL LOVE
I'M A JEWEL, I'M A FLOWER, I'M A PETAL
I'M A GEM, I'M A PRIZE
UNDT SO DAINTY FOR MY SIZE
I'M A CUTIE, I'M A BEAUTY, I'M THEIR GRETEL!

(*She whirls around oohing and aahing over the flowers and
manages to knock down one row of SUITORS after
another. The PARENTS tumble next, and after ALL pick
themselves up, the DANCE begins. A clog for MRS. YEA-
MONS, SUITORS, DUTCH GIRLS, HARRIGAN, and
HART, building to climax as they all sweep down to foot-
lights. Last pose, applause, and number ends.*)

[MUSIC NO. 13A: GRETEL BOWS]

(*LIGHT effect as they take their bows. First SUITORS and
DUTCH GIRLS, then MRS. YEAMONS, and finally
HARRIGAN and HART. Huge ovation through which we
begin to hear cries of "Author! Author! Ned! Ned!" TONY
hears them too. HARRIGAN is aware of TONY's feelings*)

but powerless to do anything but accept the cheers as TONY bows and goes smiling offstage leaving him alone. A last bow, and HARRIGAN hurries off as waltz MUSIC comes up.)

[MUSIC NO. 13B: RESTAURANT WALTZ:]

(*Two DANCERS cross the floor, and we find ourselves in. . . .*)

SCENE 9

An elegant restaurant *later that night. TONY HART, NAT GOODWIN, the two girls, BELLE and GERTA GRAN-VILLE. GOODWIN is talking to a waiter.*

NAT. No, another big one, what's it called—A magnum! Why not? It's an opening night. And what an opening! Did you hear them, Tony?

TONY HART. (*already quite high*) I heard.

NAT. Then drink up, boy! Celebrate! You've struck it rich! Look at him, ladies, best catch in town—Not you, Belle, I said ladies.

BELLE. And what am I, pray, if not? Regard this frock, for instance. Imported Belgian lace and there ain't nothin' more genteel. In fact I'm lace. . . . (*She hiccups.*) From the butt up.

NAT. (*swiftly*) Come on, let's dance. (*And he hauls her up and off to the dance floor. TONY pours another glass of wine for himself.*)

TONY HART. I like Belle. She's nice.

GERTA. I'm sure she is. (*putting her hand over her glass as TONY starts to fill it*) No more for me, thank you. (*He starts to pour anyway, she pulls her hand away.*) Really, Mr. Hart, I. . . .

TONY HART. (*mumbling on*) She likes me and I like her. Nat likes me too. (*He drains the glass.*) A lot of people like me.

GERTA. You shouldn't drink your champagne that way, Mr. Hart. It's meant to be sipped like this.

TONY HART. Ned doesn't though.

GERTA. Ned?

TONY HART. (*impatiently*) Ned, Ned! Didn't you hear tonight? We want Ned, Ned! Ned used to like me but he doesn't anymore. (*pouring champagne*) And don't tell me how to drink champagne, Miss whatever-your-name-is. I paid for it and I'll drink it my way.

GERTA. I'm not telling you how to drink champagne, Mr. Hart, I only pointed out that. . . .

TONY HART. Shut up. We're talking about Ned. And even though he doesn't like me anymore, I like him. Only he shouldn't have done all this. Building the theatre, hiring all those people, getting married. (*He knocks over his glass. The wine splashes on GERTA's dress.*)

GERTA. (*standing*) Mr. Hart, if you don't have some black coffee or eat something I shall have to. . . .

TONY HART. All right, I'll eat something, I'll eat you! (*He laughs.*) I'll put you on a piece of toast and eat you all up even the fingernails. (*GERTA turns away.*) You don't think that's funny, do you. I heard Nat say it once to this girl Lola Leary and she thought it was funny only when I say it I guess it's different.

GERTA. Really, Mr. Hart, I find this conversation quite pointless.

TONY HART. You know what, so do I. Poor Tony Hart. No friend, no girl, no. . . . (*hiccup*) point. (*GERTA rises.*) Where are you going?

GERTA. Home, Mr. Hart.

TONY HART. Why?

GERTA. Because if I stay I might be tempted to say some things you wouldn't like hearing.

TONY HART. (*as she starts up*) Like what?

GERTA. Some other time, Mr. Hart.

TONY HART. (*imitating her*) Some other time, Mr. Hart! (*grabbing her wrist*) Look, Miss Granville, or whatever-your-name-is, you're getting a free meal out of this and you'll answer when you're told. Like what! (*He is obviously hurting her. After a long moment:*)

GERTA. Isn't it obvious? The way you go on about your beloved Ned, your drunkenness, your brutality to women. You're not much of a man. (*TONY drops her wrist.*)

TONY HART. What do you mean?

GERTA. I think I've made myself clear, Mr. Hart.

TONY HART. Look, if you think I haven't had women, you're wrong! I've had 'em. Hundreds of them.

GERTA. Like Belle? For a free meal or perhaps something more? Try a real woman sometime, Mr. Hart. It might do wonders for you.

TONY HART. I don't need a woman. I don't need anybody.

GERTA. (*shaking her head, smiling*) Don't you, Mr. Hart? [MUSIC NO. 14: WHAT YOU NEED IS A WOMAN] Oh dear, I'm afraid I'm going to make you angry again because, you see. . . . (*softly*) I think you do. (*And she sings.*)
WHAT YOU NEED IS A WOMAN
WITH ALL SHE BRINGS A MAN
ONE WHO'S THERE TO COMFORT HIM
ANY WAY SHE CAN

WHAT YOU NEED IS HER CALMNESS
WITH ALL THAT WORD IMPLIES
A CALM TO SOOTHE THE SORROW
SHE MIGHT NOTICE IN YOUR EYES

A MAN MAY HAVE THE PROMISE
TO DO WHAT HE MUST DO
BUT IT TAKES A WOMAN'S WISDOM
TO SEE HIS PROMISE THROUGH

THE PEACE OF MIND THAT HE LONGS FOR
THE GOAL HE'S DREAMING OF
CAN BE HIS WHEN HE HAS A WOMAN
A WOMAN
TO LOVE . . .
(*Through last of this, GERTA has put on her gloves, now rises as MUSIC continues.*) I daresay I've said enough for one evening. Will you get a hack for me, Mr. Hart, or shall I do it myself?

TONY HART. My. . . . my carriage is outside. I'll take you home.

GERTA. That's not necessary, Mr. Hart. I'm sure you'd rather stay here and. . . .

TONY HART. I said I'll take you home!

GERTA. (*softly*) Very well, Mr. Hart. You may take me home. (*As TONY goes off to get her wrap:*)
A MAN MAY HAVE THE PROMISE
TO DO WHAT HE MUST DO
BUT IT TAKES A WOMAN'S WISDOM
TO SEE HIS PROMISE THROUGH

YES, WHAT YOU NEED IS A WOMAN
THAT'S VERY PLAIN TO SEE

AS A MATTER OF FACT, A WOMAN
A WOMAN . . .
(*LIGHTS have irised down to GERTA's face, a thoughtful look in her eyes, the hint of a smile on her lips.*)
LIKE ME.

(*By now LIGHTS are out and we are up on. . . .*)

[MUSIC NO. 14A: MYSTIC STAR/SCENE OPENING]

SCENE 10

Stage of Comique Theatre. *Direct overlap from applause of previous scene as first ONE DANCER, then ANOTHER, then ANOTHER comes onstage doing the same precision step until an entire SEXTETTE is dancing to the music of "Mystic Star" played on rehearsal piano. Two-thirds of the way through chorus they are interrupted by the arrival of TONY HART, followed at a slight distance by GERTA GRANVILLE, as he bursts on.*

TONY HART. I know I'm late — one hour and thirty-five minutes to be exact — but for once I have a good excuse! Ned, Annie, Martin, everybody, I want you to meet a very special visitor — Miss Gerta Granville of London, England, who as of this very day, is engaged to be married to that former reprobate, loafer, man-about-town and general ne'er-do-well — Mr. Tony Hart!

ALL. (*variously*) Tony! What? Hooray! Congratulations, Tony, she's gorgeous! Etc.

ANNIE HARRIGAN. (*crossing to GERTA*) Miss Granville, I'm so pleased for you!

GERTA. Thank you, Mrs. Harrigan. I know it's all very sudden but Tony just swept me off my feet.

ANNIE HARRIGAN. Please, I'm Annie! And that's Harry, and Jennie, and Johnny, and Sam — and here's another Annie — Annie Yeamons.

MRS. YEAMONS. Put 'er there, Gert. (*They all laugh, GERTA smiles, introductions continue round the company as NED draws TONY aside.*)

HARRIGAN. Tony, why didn't you tell me?

TONY HART. Why, Ned? Don't you approve?

HARRIGAN. Of course I approve. She's lovely! But I would like to have known.

TONY HART. Can't I have some secrets, Ned? I'm sure you do. By the way, Gerta's an actress.

HARRIGAN. Is she? Then she'll join the company! A pretty girl like that's just what we need.

TONY HART. Gerta'll be pleased to hear that, Ned. She thought you might not want her.

HARRIGAN. Might not want her? Why?

TONY HART. Oh, the others. They might be jealous. She didn't dare ask herself, she spent half the morning saying, "Now, Tony, just remember who you are and insist."

HARRIGAN. Have you ever had to insist, Tony?

TONY HART. No, but I haven't been much of a partner, have I? That's why Gerta'll be such a help to me, she can look out for my interests.

HARRIGAN. I didn't know they'd been neglected.

TONY HART. It's not that, Ned, but Gerta says I'm letting you down if I don't consider my importance to the company. If my name's up there with yours, I've got to make it mean something. That's what Gerta says. (*NED doesn't answer.*) You do like her, don't you, Ned?

HARRIGAN. Of course. Of course, I do! Now you tell her to come back early this afternoon and we'll see what we can work out for her in the new show. How about Rose, the Widow Nolan's daughter! We could change it a little, have her educated in England, that'll explain the accent, and. . . .

ANNIE HARRIGAN. (*coming over*) Look at the two of them! Talking business at a time like this. Now why don't we all go out to lunch together — Mr. Harrigan's treat — And celebrate!

GERTA. I'd love to, Mrs. Harrigan — Annie — but I have an appointment at the dressmaker. But I'll be back first thing this afternoon. Tony's going to talk about my roles and I certainly want to be there.

HARRIGAN. Won't be necessary! We've talked already and your roles are all set.

GERTA. Well, really, I rather thought I. . . .

HARRIGAN. You're to have whatever parts you want! Men's parts excepted of course. Just look over the script and take your choice.

GERTA. Tony!

TONY HART. It was Ned's idea, Gerta.

GERTA. I know better. But now I'll have to show you that I can really do it. It's all very well for Tony to insist—after all he *is* half this company—but it's up to me to prove myself. Now what time are we due back, Mr. Harrigan?

HARRIGAN. After lunch. Two o'clock.

GERTA. Two sharp then. I'm a demon on punctuality. Goodbye, Annie, everybody. Tony, will you see me out?

TONY HART. Of course. Back in a minute, Ned.

GERTA. (*as she leaves with TONY*) Au revoir. 'Til two. (*And they are gone. A moment, then MRS. YEAMONS turns to ADA LEWIS.*)

MRS. YEAMONS. Au revoir! 'Til two! Did you hear that voice? Scratch it and you'll find a good helping of plain Brooklyn if you ask me!

HARRIGAN. Annie! Miss Granville was just trying to be nice. It's not easy meeting all of you at once, you know. And she's a lady.

MRS. YEAMONS. (*aside*) So's my old man.

HARRIGAN. All right, all right, let's get on with it. I want to continue with Mrs. Yeamons' song!

MRS. YEAMONS. Mine for the time being.

HARRIGAN. With Mrs. Yeamons' song! And, Dave, keep the tempo bright, it's the end of Act I, I want to leave them buzzing for the intermission.

[MUSIC NO. 15/16: MYSTIC STAR]

(*MUSIC UP as MRS. YEAMONS and SEXTETTE move forward as they sing.*)

MRS. YEAMONS, OTHERS.
WAY, WAY OVER YONDER
WHERE THE PLANETS WANDER
VENUS, AND NEPTUNE, AND JUPITER AND MARS
THERE'S ONE STAR WE SWEAR IS
QUITE THE FAIREST THERE IS
THAT'S WHY THEY CALL US, THE KNIGHTS OF THE
    MYSTIC STAR!
MRS. YEAMONS.
OH WE TALK IN A TONGUE THAT IS MYSTICAL TOO
    FOUR GIRLS.
WITH A ZIM, AND A ZUM, AND AN ALAKAZOO

MRS. YEAMONS.
FOR WE LEAD SUCH A MYSTIC LIFE
OTHERS.
WITH OUR MYSTIC LITTLE KIDDIES
AND A MYSTICAL WIFE!
MRS. YEAMONS.
OH WE DANCE ALL ALONE WITH A MYSTICAL HOP
OTHERS.
WHILE THE PUP CHEWS THE BONE OF A MYSTICAL
CHOP
MRS. YEAMONS.
IT'S NO SECRET WHO WE ARE
WE ARE KNOWN FROM NEAR TO FAR
AS THE KNIGHTS OF THE MYSTIC STAR!
ALL.
WAY, WAY OVER YONDER
(WHERE THE PLANETS WANDER
VENUS, AND NEPTUNE, AND JUPITER AND MARS . . .)

(*Through this last a more languorous half-time tempo begins
in the orchestra as LIGHTS dim on MRS. YEAMONS and
start up on GERTA — now in a beautiful evening gown — and
two MEN in formal attire, as they start down through MRS.
YEAMONS' group, and sing.*)

GERTA. (*as MRS. YEAMONS watches from the left, shakes
her head and exits*)
WAY, WAY OVER YONDER
WHERE THE PLANETS WANDER
VENUS, AND NEPTUNE, AND JUPITER AND MARS
THERE'S ONLY ONE STAR THEY SWEAR IS
QUITE THE FAIREST THERE IS
THAT'S WHY THEY CALL ME THE GIRL OF THE
MYSTIC STAR
(*spot irises down on GERTA as she sings*)
THERE'S ONE STAR THEY SWEAR IS
QUITE THE FAIREST THERE IS
THAT'S WHY
THEY CALL ME
THE GIRL OF THE MYSTIC STAR.

GERTA.	MEN.
THERE'S ONE STAR THEY	THERE'S . . .

SWEAR IS
QUITE THE FAIREST   QUITE THE FAIREST
  THERE IS   THERE IS
THAT'S WHY
THEY CALL ME
THE GIRL OF THE   GIRL OF THE MYSTIC
  MYSTIC STAR.   STAR.

TONY HART. (D.R. *with NED as GERTA and MEN continue dance off* L.) They don't like Gerta, Ned. She says almost nobody in the company speaks to her.

HARRIGAN. She's new, Tony. It takes time for them to warm up.

TONY HART. Hello and goodbye, that's all they say. Even Annie.

HARRIGAN. Annie Yeamons does not run this company and it's high time she. . . .

TONY HART. *Your* Annie, Ned. Annie Harrigan. Gerta says you know about it or she wouldn't dare.

HARRIGAN. (*angrily*) That's ridiculous! You tell Gerta that. . . .

TONY HART. Tell Gerta what, Ned? (*MUSIC fades.*)

HARRIGAN. That. . . . (*controlling himself*) That I'll speak to Annie. It won't happen again.

TONY HART. Thank you, Ned.

HARRIGAN. (*TONY has started away.*) Tony! (*He stops.*) If our wives have words—and wives sometimes do—it's their words, not ours.

TONY HART. I hope so, Ned.

HARRIGAN. How can you think anything else? You're my partner! Without Hart there is no Harrigan. God help me, Tony, but there's not anyone in this world means anything to me before you!

TONY HART. Except Annie and the kids.

HARRIGAN. I said not anyone, Tony! God help me.

TONY HART. (*realizing what it has meant for NED to say this*) I'm sorry, Ned. I shouldn't have brought it up. It's Gerta. She's . . . . she's nervous.

HARRIGAN. She doesn't have to be, Tony! They'll like her if she gives them a chance.

TONY HART. It's just that there's so many of them. Everywhere she turns there's a Harrigan or a Braham.

HARRIGAN. And what about Uncle Albert? (*A MAN has wandered on through this. He smokes a pipe, carries a gas work light.*) He's worth all the Harrigans put together. Comes an hour late, leaves an hour early. He's no comfort to Gerta though, he doesn't talk to anyone. (*putting his arm around TONY's shoulder*) It'll all work out, I know it will! It takes time, that's all.

TONY HART. I'll tell her, Ned. I'll ask her to be patient. (*He starts off.*) It was better before, you know.

[MUSIC NO. 17: MULLIGAN GUARD REPRISE/END ACT I]

HARRIGAN. Before?

TONY HART. Before the theatre, the company, all this. Just the two of us, Ned. Just you and me. (*And softly at first, a cappella, TONY sings.*)
WE CRAVE YOUR CONDESCENSION
TO TELL YOU WHAT WE KNOW
OF MARCHING IN THE MULLIGAN GUARD
FROM BAXTER STREET BELOW . . .
HARRIGAN. (*joining him, as MUSIC comes softly up*)
OUR CAPTAIN'S NAME WAS HUSSEY
A TIPPERARY MAN
HE CARRIED HIS SWORD LIKE A RUSSIAN DUKE
WHENEVER HE TOOK COMMAND

(*TONY and NED automatically go into their marching routine as NED shouts,* "Right face! Left face! About face! Hold your face!" *and then into the Mulligan Guard Dance. Dance ends as they both sing.*)

HARRIGAN & HART.
WE SHOULDERED ARMS
AND MARCHED AND MARCHED AWAY
FROM BAXTER STREET
WE MARCHED TO AVENUE A . . .
(*They joke with each other as they start off up right.*)
WITH DRUMS AND FIFE
HOW SWEETLY THEY DID PLAY
AS WE MARCHED, MARCHED, MARCHED
IN THE MULLIGAN . . .
MARCHED, MARCHED, MARCHED
IN THE MULLIGAN . . .

(*MUSIC fades as they go off together, arms over each other's shoulders. A moment as we become aware of WATCH-*

MAN still on stage. He slowly crosses D.R. *and knocks the cinders of his pipe in wastebasket then puts on his coat and starts out. LIGHTS have come down through this, VOICES of TONY and NED still faintly audible in distance. Last spot holds on wastebasket as thin curl of smoke starts from it. Smoke grows thicker, spot glows redder and redder as sound of horse-drawn fire engine is heard in distance. It draws closer and closer, becoming almost deafening in its volume—then a sudden cutoff of siren and LIGHTS, as CURTAIN comes down on. . . .)*

END OF ACT I

ACT TWO

Scene 1

[MUSIC NO. 18: ENTR'ACTE]

*A conventional ENTR'ACTE ending with sound of fire sirens
fading in distance as we come up on TONY HART and
GERTA down right. TONY wears coat hastily thrown over
his night clothes. A deep red glow in sky behind them.
NEWSPAPERMAN talking to GERTA as TONY stares at
the red sky upstage.*

NEWSPAPERMAN. . . . I know the loss of the theatre is a great
shock, Mr. Hart, but there are certain questions the public will
want answered. This watchman — the one who was supposed to
be at the theatre all night — he's an uncle of yours, isn't he?

GERTA. Who told you that? (*before NEWSPAPERMAN can
answer*) Mr. Harrigan, I daresay. Or Mr. Hanley. Well you can
tell your readers the watchman *is* a relative of Mr. Hart's but
that had nothing to do with the fire.

NEWSPAPERMAN. Perhaps not with the fire itself, but if he
hadn't left early it might have been put out on time. Mr. Hanley
said. . . .

GERTA. I thought so. What did Mr. Hanley say?

NEWSPAPERMAN. Nothing. Just that the fire must have started
about seven in the evening and if the watchman had stayed the
theatre might have been saved.

GERTA. Well as long as you're collecting "ifs" how about this
one. If Mr. Harrigan's insurance broker — and brother-in-law —
hadn't let the insurance policy lapse only last week, there might
have been some hope of building a new theatre! But I daresay
Mr. Hanley didn't mention that.

[MUSIC NO. 19: SKIDMORE FANCY BALL]

(*As MUSIC comes up, SAM NICHOLS, HARRY MACK,
JOHNNY WILD, BILLY GROSS, start on. NOTE: During
following, through use of minimal scenic effects, we learn
that songs that separate these short scenes are part of the*

56

farewell performance at the Park Theatre, two weeks hence.)

TONY HART. Gerta, please.

GERTA. (*imitating him*) Gerta, please! How long are you going to let them walk all over us? They're blaming the fire on you!

TONY HART. I'm sure Ned doesn't think I. . . .

GERTA. Well, I'm not! And if you don't print your side of the story, all New York will be blaming you too.

TONY HART. (*as they exit and number takes over the stage*) All right, Gerta. But I still don't think Ned would. . . .

QUARTETTE.
PUT ON YOUR BEST
EMBROIDERED VEST
YOUR TIE AND TAILS AND ALL
THEN SHINE EACH SHOE
AND HEAD RIGHT TO
THE SKIDMORE FANCY BALL

WE'LL DIP AND WING
THEN U-UP WE'LL SPRING
AND FLING OUR PARTNERS ROUND
WE'LL DO THE WALTZ
WITH SOMERSAULTS
THEN TOSS THEM OFF THE GROUND
WE'LL SLIP AND SLIDE
THEN OVER WE'LL GLIDE
AND PRANCE RIGHT UP THE WALL
ALL IN A TRANCE
THAT'S HO-OW WE DANCE
AT THE SKIDMORE FANCY BALL!

[MUSIC NO. 19A: SKIDMORE UNDERSCORE]

HARRIGAN. (*as QUARTETTE continues number off*) Of course it's ridiculous! They make it sound as if Tony were accusing me!

ANNIE HARRIGAN. In a way he is, Ned.

HARRIGAN. You don't understand newspapermen, Annie. They take what you say and twist it and . . .

ANNIE HARRIGAN. (*reading*) "Mr. Hart also said that if Mr. Harrigan's brother-in-law hadn't let the insurance policy lapse just the week before, a new Comique could have been built at once." (*putting down paper as Skidmore QUARTETTE goes off*) That's fairly clear.

(*ELSIE FAY and ADA LEWIS start on, dressed for their song as two street urchins.*)

HARRIGAN. It's all a misunderstanding! I know it is! I'll go and see Tony.

ANNIE HARRIGAN. I suppose you'd better — but not right now. Wait till things cool down, another day or two.

[MUSIC NO. 20: LOVE SWEETEST LOVE]

(*And by now they are off as ELSIE and ADA sing:*)

ELSIE & ADA.
LOVE LOVE SWEETEST LOVE
NOW OPE YOUR WINDOW WIDE
LOOK DOWN FROM UP ABOVE
UPON A GENTLE BRIDE

SING SING GAILY SING
TRUE LOVE WILL NEVER FADE
SWEET MELODY WE SING TO THEE
NOW IN OUR SERENADE.

TONY HART. (*as ELSIE FAY and ADA continue dancing off*) Ned hasn't come by?

GERTA. Did you expect him to?

TONY HART. Yes, Gerta, I did.

GERTA. Well I'm afraid you're in for a disappointment. Word has it your dear partner is furious. Why? Because for once in your life you didn't let him walk all over you. (*TONY has started off.*) Where are you going?

TONY HART. To see Ned. Explain.

GERTA. And as much as admit the fire was your fault? No, my dear, if your beloved partner has your interests so much at heart he'll come to see you.

TONY HART. (*By now, ELSIE and ADA are off, and FOX, JENNIE YEAMONS, JOHNNY WILD and LILY FAY come on.*) Gerta, don't do this. Don't start something we can't stop. . . .

GERTA. I'm starting nothing. I'm only trying to get you to face facts. Or are you afraid to put Mr. Ned Harrigan's great devotion to the test?

TONY HART. I'm not afraid of anything, I just don't want to. . . .

[MUSIC NO. 21: OLD BARN FLOOR]

(*As they exit and FOX, JENNY YEAMONS, JOHNNY WILD and LILY FAY start down.*) All right, Gerta. I'll wait.

ALL FOUR.
EV'RY NIGHT AT EIGHT
WHEN THE OLD BARN GATE
I-IS SHUT TILL THE DAWN DOTH BREAK
WHEN THE COWS AND SHEEP
OUGHT TO BE ASLEEP
THEY ARE ALL QUITE WIDE AWAKE
THERE'S AN OLD BLACK CROW
WITH A BIG BANJO
AND HE STRUMS A QUICK TWO-FOUR
WHILE EACH HEN AND PIG
STARTS TO REEL AND JIG
AS THEY DANCE ON THE OLD BARN FLOOR
WITH A QUACK QUACK QUACK QUACK CHICK CHICK
   CHICK
THEY HOP AND SKIP AND GLIDE
WITH A MOO MOO MOO MOO OINK OINK OINK
THEY DIP AND SLIP AND SLIDE
WITH A HEE-HAW HEE-HAW CLUCK CLUCK CLUCK
AS THEY BEG FOR JUST ONE MORE
WITH A COCK-A-DOODLE-DO, DOODLE-DO,
   DOODLE-DO
(*Variously*) QUACK QUACK, CHICK CHICK, MOO MOO,
   OINK!
THEY DANCE ON THE OLD BARN FLOOR!

MARTIN HANLEY. (*As FOURSOME continue their step off*) All right, go to him if you want, Ned, but it's as much as admitting you can't do without him.

HARRIGAN. Martin, I can't!

HANLEY. That's ridiculous. The boy's talented, yes, but a dozen youngsters could do his parts. It's the words that matter!

HARRIGAN. Maybe a dozen could do them, but none like Tony! I'll go this afternoon.

HANLEY. Wait a minute, Ned, at least do this on a business basis! Have a meeting. Here, in the office.

HARRIGAN. (*As FOURSOME exits and GERTA, in showy calf-length flare skirt, comes on with BILLY GROSS rather foppishly done up a la Little Lord Fauntleroy.*) Why must it be so formal? Isn't it easier to go over to Tony's — right now — and tell him I want him back!

HANLEY. Believe me, Ned, there's a way to handle these things. Send Tony a wire. [MUSIC NO. 22: SILLY BOY] Ask him to be at the office ten tomorrow morning. It's the best way, Ned. The best way.

GERTA. (*as GROSS promenades on her arm*)
OH ISN'T HE A DEAR
A PROPER MAMMA'S PET
SO QUICK TO SHED A TEAR
IF HE SHOULD BE UPSET
HE WEARS A SHIRT OF LACE
AND CUFFS OF VELVETEEN
AND ALL THE LADIES THINK HE IS
THE SWEETEST THING THEY'VE SEEN

SILLY BOY
MAMMA'S JOY
WITH AN AIR
OH SO RARE
EVEN CHAPS
LIFT THEIR CAPS
FOR THEY THINK HE'S SO DIVINE
DAINTY CURLS
THAT THE GIRLS
WISH THEY HAD
BUT HOW SAD
FOR YOU SEE
LUCKY ME
THAT POOR SILLY BOY IS MINE
(*as HARRY MACK comes on as POLICEMAN*)
A SERGEANT OF POLICE
UPON A MUDDY DAY
MADE ALL THE TRAFFIC CEASE
SO HE COULD CROSS BROADWAY
THE SERGEANT SAID, "MY BOY
HOW ODDLY DO YOU DRESS
AND THOUGH I DON'T APPROVE AT ALL

PLEASE GIVE ME YOUR ADDRESS."
(*as MEN join GERTA*)

GERTA. (*continued*)	GROSS AND MACK.
SILLY BOY	SILLY BOY
MAMMA'S JOY	
WITH AN AIR	WITH AN AIR
OH SO RARE	
EVEN CHAPS	CHAPS
LIFT THEIR CAPS	LIFT THEIR CAPS
FOR THEY THINK	
HE'S SO DIVINE	
DAINTY CURLS	DAINTY CURLS
THAT THE GIRLS	
WISH THEY HAD	WISH THEY HAD
BUT HOW SAD	BUT HOW SAD
FOR YOU SEE	FOR YOU SEE
LUCKY ME . . .	

GERTA. (*a very slow smile*)
THAT POOR SILLY BOY IS MINE.

(*GERTA continues* U.R., *puts on coat over her costume as MEN continue step and NED and TONY start on. A moment, then TONY runs to him.*)

HARRIGAN. Tony!

TONY HART. (*as HARRIGAN embraces him*) Ned! Ned, I. . . .

HARRIGAN. Look, Tony, I know we're all supposed to sit down and discuss this on a business basis but before we start I want you to know I think it's a fuss over nothing! Who cares whose fault it was? Your uncle, my brother-in-law. . . .

GERTA. (*now wearing coat, moving into scene*) Tony understands that, Mr. Harrigan. What's upsetting him is the things you said about anyone being able to do his parts.

HARRIGAN. I didn't quite say it that way, Mrs. Hart. I said anyone can do them but no one like Tony!

GERTA. But anyone can do them.

HARRIGAN. No one is indispensable, Mrs. Hart. Including me. But there's no one can do the things we do better than the way we do them!

GERTA. You think a lot of yourself, don't you, Mr. Harrigan.

HARRIGAN. I think a lot of both of us!

GERTA. Enough to put it to the test?

HARRIGAN. What are you talking about? Tony, can't we just talk alone, just the two of us.

GERTA. (*overriding him*) I'm talking about going on by yourself if you're so confident, Mr. Harrigan.

HARRIGAN. Look, Mrs. Hart, I suggest you stop this before I say a few things I'm going to be sorry about! I don't want to go on by myself, I want Tony! Is that clear?

GERTA. I didn't come here to be shouted at, Mr. Harrigan.

HARRIGAN. You didn't come here to patch things up between Tony and me either! Now if you'll all just let us alone, we'll work things out by ourselves.

GERTA. The way you've worked them out before, Mr. Harrigan? Your way?

HARRIGAN. Tony!

TONY HART. You mustn't shout at Gerta, Ned, she's only trying to. . . .

HARRIGAN. I'm not shouting, I'm just trying to get you to understand that I want my partner! Without Hart there is no Harrigan!

GERTA. Words, Mr. Harrigan. Getting us nowhere as usual. If you want my suggestion, a cooling-off period might be in order.

HARRIGAN. Fine, a little walk around the block, fifteen minutes then we can. . . .

GERTA. I meant longer than that, Mr. Harrigan. A few months. Time to let things quiet down.

HARRIGAN. (*as drum pulse starts*) What are you talking about?

TONY HART. A little vacation, Ned. Gerta and I discussed it last night. Then in the Fall we can. . . .

HARRIGAN. The Fall? We're booked at the Park Theatre next week. A signed contract!

TONY HART. He's right, Gerta. I'd forgotten all about it.

GERTA. And what about "Buttons." It's a new play, Mr. Harrigan. Written especially for Tony by William Gill, the dramatist. You see, despite the prevailing opinion Tony thinks he can make it on his own.

HARRIGAN. I don't understand. You're going to open in a new play?

TONY HART. Gerta found it, Ned. In a way it'll be good for both of us. Make us appreciate each other twice as much when we come back together. And don't worry, we can still play the Park date. It's only two weeks. Gerta.

HARRIGAN. Wait a minute. A new play doesn't get written in a week. How long has this been going on?

GERTA. I commissioned it some time ago, Mr. Harrigan. When I first realized my husband couldn't go on playing second fiddle.

HARRIGAN. Martin, we'd better go.

HANLEY. Very well, Ned.

HARRIGAN. Goodbye, Tony. I don't imagine we'll need much rehearsal for the Park Theatre. Say two days before. Good day, Mrs. Hart. And my congratulations. You've done what you set out to do! Come along, Martin.

(*Through above, one by one, COMPANY has come on and now as proscenium and backdrop come in we realize that we are at that final performance at the* Park Theatre, Brooklyn.)

GERTA. Did you ever hear such rudeness! He practically accused me of. . . . Where are you going?

TONY HART. I didn't say goodbye to Ned.

GERTA. Goodbye to him? After the way he insulted me?

TONY HART. You don't understand, Gerta.

GERTA. No, I don't understand. You see, I thought I married a man.

TONY HART. Don't start that again, Gerta.

GERTA. I don't mind being disappointed in some respects but in public I would appreciate your acting like a man and not some lovesick little girl.

TONY HART. Stop it, Gerta!

GERTA. Some lovesick little girl who goes running after the man who insults his wife! Well, what are you waiting for? Run after him, darling! Run! (*TONY suddenly slaps her. A moment, then:*)

TONY HART. Gerta. . . . Gerta, I'm sorry. . . . Gerta, please . . . . Gerta. . . .

[MUSIC NO. 23: MULLIGAN GUARD FULL COMPANY REPRISE]

(*By now ENTIRE COMPANY has assembled, LIGHTS up on finale of that last number in last performance, as they sing.*)

ENTIRE COMPANY. (*joined by HARRIGAN and HART in*

Mulligan Guard costumes, full performance smiles over the tension underneath)
WE SHOULDERED ARMS
AND MARCHED AND MARCHED AWAY
FROM BAXTER STREET
WE MARCHED TO AVENUE A
WITH DRUMS AND FIFES
HOW SWEETLY THEY DID PLAY
AS WE MARCHED, MARCHED, MARCHED
TO THE MULLIGAN GUARD!

(*Dance Interlude with Mulligan Guard step for ENTIRE COMPANY, ending as the* Park Theatre *begins to be stripped away and they sing.*)
WITH DRUMS AND FIFE
WE SHOULDERED AND MARCHED
AS WE MARCHED, MARCHED, MARCHED IN THE
    MULLIGAN
(*MUSIC as members of COMPANY begin breaking out of formation, passing the news of the breakup among each other.*)
MARCHED, MARCHED, MARCHED IN THE MULLIGAN
MARCHED, MARCHED, MARCHED IN THE MULLIGAN
MARCHED, MARCHED, MARCHED IN THE MULLIGAN
MARCHED, MARCHED, MARCHED IN THE
    MULLIGAN . . .

(*By now protesting COMPANY is around TONY and NED until finally HARRIGAN makes himself heard above them.*)

HARRIGAN. Only a temporary separation! A few months, that's all, then we'll be back together again! (*COMPANY variously shouting,* "No, no!") Back together again bigger and better than ever, the way it's always been. . . . (*His arm is around TONY's shoulder.*) Tony and Ned, Tony and Ned! You don't think we could give all this up, do you? (*Noise is abating.*) The sight of all your faces, the feel of being beside you night after night for all these happy years. (*There is silence.*) And the sounds. [MUSIC NO. 24: WE'LL BE THERE] (*He looks at the empty theatre around them.*) The sweet familiar sounds, of this blessed place. (*And, ad-lib at first, he sings.*)
THERE'S A WHIR FROM THE WIND IN THE ALLEY
THERE'S A CLANK FROM THE LATCH ON THE DOOR

THERE'S A TICK FROM THE CLOCK BY THE
   CALLBOARD
AND A SQUEAK FROM THE CRACKS ON THE FLOOR
(*Rhythm softly sneaks in.*)
THERE'S A PURR FROM THE CAT IN THE BASEMENT
MAKING MUSIC FOR THE MAGIC IN THE AIR
AND WE'LL BE THERE!
WE'LL BE THERE!

   TONY HART.

THERE'S A CLANG FROM THE PIPE ON THE CEILING
THERE'S A CREAK FROM THE DRESSING ROOM CHAIR
THERE'S A BUZZ FROM THE FLY IN THE GREASEPAINT
AND A HUM FROM THE DRAFT ON THE STAIR

   HARRIGAN & HART.

THERE'S A SQUEAL FROM THE ROPE PULLIN' SCEN'RY
MAKING MUSIC FOR THE MAGIC IN THE AIR
AND WE'LL BE THERE!
WE'LL BE THERE!

(*By ones, by twos, the other members of the COMPANY begin
to join them until ALL are singing.*)

   MRS. YEAMONS.

THERE'S A RING FROM THE BELL IN THE LOBBY

   MRS. YEAMONS AND ANNIE.

THERE'S A CLINK FROM THE CRYSTAL CHANDELIER

   LILY, ADA, GROSS, FOX.

THERE'S APPLAUSE FROM THE FOLKS IN THE BOXES

   ALL PRINCIPALS.

AS THE FELLAS IN THE ORCHESTRA APPEAR

   COMPANY.

THERE'S A FLAP FROM THE FOLDS OF THE CURTAIN
MAKING MUSIC FOR THE MAGIC IN THE AIR
AND WE'LL BE THERE!
YOU KNOW WE'LL BE THERE!
WE'LL BE THERE, WE'LL BE THERE!

   HARRIGAN & HART AND COMPANY.

THERE'S A RING FROM THE BELL IN THE LOBBY
THERE'S A CLINK FROM THE CRYSTAL CHANDELIER
THERE'S APPLAUSE FROM THE FOLKS IN THE BOXES
AS THE FELLAS IN THE ORCHESTRA APPEAR
THERE'S A FLAP FROM THE FOLDS OF THE CURTAIN
MAKING MUSIC FOR THE MAGIC IN THE AIR

(*MUSIC continues as members of the COMPANY circle round*

D.S. *of TONY and NED and salute them with the same little*
pantomimic signature they gave on their first entrances.
When ALL have passed, they sing.)

AND WE'LL BE THERE IN STEP
WE'LL BE THERE ON KEY
WE'LL BE THERE IN TUNE AND ON TRACK
PUTTING WORDS TO THE MUSIC
  Hart.
HARRIGAN & HART!
  Harrigan.
HARRIGAN & HART!
  Others.
HARRIGAN & HART!
  All.
ARE BACK!

(*TONY and NED join hands triumphantly as number ends.*
[music no. 24a: we'll be there playoff] *Applause, and as*
MUSIC softly continues, members of the COMPANY start
off. There should be a great sadness, a feeling of perma-
nence about the parting, that permeates this. Finally only
TONY and NED are left. NED puts his arms out to TONY.
TONY tries to reach out to him, can't, slowly puts down his
arms, turns and exits L. *A moment, NED takes a deep breath*
and exits swiftly R. *and we come up on. . . .*) [music no. 25:
ada]

Scene 2

Olios that roll down to show HARRIGAN's progress over the
next five years as he takes his company out without TONY
HART. The first of the Olios is the program for "The Last
Of The Hogans" *starring EDWARD HARRIGAN and fea-*
turing ANNIE HARRIGAN, BILLY GROSS, and JOHNNY
WILD as they sing.

Billy Gross and Johnny Wild. (*as ANNIE HARRIGAN*
promenades between them)
OH HOW I LOVE MY ADA
CHARMING LITTLE ADA

FRISKY LITTLE ADA
OH HOW I LOVE MY ADA
ADA WITH THE GOLDEN HAIR
   ANNIE HARRIGAN. (*as WILD and GROSS, quietly at first,
begin fighting over her*)
WE SAT BY THE RIVER YOU AND I
IN THE SWEET SUMMERTIME LONG AGO
SO SMOOTHLY THE WATER GLIDED BY
MAKING MUSIC IN ITS TRANQUIL FLOW
   ALL THREE. (*as boys begin pulling ANNIE from side to side*)
SINGING ADA!
SWEET ADA!
ADA WITH THE GOLDEN HAIR
ADA!
SWEET ADA!
ADA WITH THE GOLDEN HAIR!
   WILD AND GROSS. (*by now down to fisticuffs*)
OH HOW I LOVE MY ADA
CHARMING LITTLE ADA
FRISKY LITTLE ADA
OH HOW I LOVE MY ADA . . .

(*They have now lifted ANNIE, stretched her between them, and
   carry her off as they sing:*)

   ALL THREE.
ADA WITH THE GOLDEN HAIR!

[MUSIC NO. 26: FEATHER BED]

(*Second Olio of* "Old Lavender" *starring EDWARD HARRI-
   GAN with HARRY MACK and the FAY SISTERS, as they
   sing:*)

   HARRY MACK.
IN THE COUNTY MAYO,
A LONG TIME AGO
ME FATHER HIMSELF TOOK A WIFE
'TWAS ALL UNDERSTOOD
HE WOULD DO WHAT HE COULD
TO PROVIDE FOR ME MOTHER THROUGH LIFE
HIS FATHER WAS FAIR,
FOR HE GAVE THEM A CHAIR

AND A TABLE TO EAT OF THEIR BREAD
HER MOTHER, GOD SAVE 'ER,
SAID ALL SHE COULD LAVE 'HER
AS A TOKEN OF LOVE
  WAS HER OLD FEATHER BED

ME FATHER AND MOTHER
ME SISTER AND BROTHER
ME GRANNY AND AUNTY
  AND BIG COUSIN TED
ME UNCLE A SAILOR
HIS NEPHEW A TAILOR
THEY ALL OF THEM SLEPT
  ON THAT BIG FEATHER BED!
  FAY SISTERS. (*faster*)
A COUSIN NAMED BARNEY
WHO CAME FROM KILLARNEY
THE BROTHER-IN-LAW
  OF MY DEAR UNCLE FRED
THE WHOLE DARN CABOODLE
TWO CATS AND A POODLE
THEY ALL OF THEM SLEPT
  ON THAT BIG FEATHER BED!
  HARRY MACK & FAY SISTERS. (*by now at top speed*)
A FRIEND OF MY BROTHER
HIS WIFE AND HER MOTHER
ME FAT COUSIN NELL
  AND THE FELLA SHE WED
AUNT PEG WHO'S A BOTHER
HER GOAT AND HER FATHER
THEY ALL OF THEM SLEPT
  ON THAT BIG FEATHER BED!!

[MUSIC NO. 27: SAM JOHNSON'S COLORED CAKEWALK]

(*Third Olio of* "Reilly and The Four Hundred" *starring ED-*
WARD HARRIGAN and featuring SAM NICHOLS and
JENNIE YEAMONS as he sings:)

  SAM NICHOLS. (*as JENNIE waltzes round him*)
ALL ROUND THE ROOM WE'RE WALTZING
LADIES AND GENTS SO SHY

WITH STEPS SO MAJESTIC, OH DEAR, OH MY
OH WHITE FOLKS, IT'S NO USE TO TRY
THIS MUSIC WOULD SET YOU DREAMING
LOVINGLY SIGH AND TALK
(*with JENNIE*)
WE'LL DANCE TILL THE MORNING IS BEAMING
(*SAM NICHOLS alone*)
AT SAM JOHNSON'S COLORED CAKEWALK.

[MUSIC NO. 28: DIP ME IN THE GOLDEN SEA]

(*Last Olio*, "Waddy Googan," *starring EDWARD HARRIGAN
and MRS. YEAMONS as they sing.*)

HARRIGAN.
OH, I LONG FOR TO REACH THAT HEAVENLY SHORE
TO DIP IN THE GOLDEN SEA!
MRS. YEAMONS.
TO MEET SAINT PETER JUST A-STANDIN' IN THE DOOR
AND DIP IN THE GOLDEN SEA!
HARRIGAN & MRS. YEAMONS.
THEN I'LL LOOK BACK DOWN ON THE WORLD BELOW
AND WATCH YOU DIGGIN' AND A-SHOVELIN' SNOW
WHILE I PLUCK MY HARP TILL IT'S TIME TO GO
AND DIP IN THE GOLDEN SEA!

SO DIP ME!
BATHE ME!
BRETHREN, YOU AND ME!
NOW YOU DON'T NEED A BOAT
CAUSE WE ALL GONNA FLOAT
WHEN WE DIP IN THE GOLDEN SEA!

SO DIP ME!
BATHE ME!
BRETHREN, YOU AND ME!
NOW YOU DON'T NEED A BOAT
CAUSE WE ALL GONNA FLOAT
WHEN WE DIP IN THE GOLDEN SEA!

(*Dance for HARRIGAN/MRS. YEAMONS/COMPANY ending with ALL onstage as they sing.*)

ALL.
SOME SUNNY DAY
WE'LL FLY, FLY AWAY (WE'LL FLY)
WITH GLADNESS AND JOY WE'LL NEVER TIRE
   (ALL FLY)
ON A SILVER CLOUD
ABOVE THE CROWD
WE'LL SING IN THE GOLDEN CHOIR

SO DIP ME! (DIP ME!)
BATHE ME! (BATHE ME!)
BRETHREN, YOU AND ME! (YOU AND ME!)
NOW YOU DON'T NEED A BOAT
CAUSE WE ALL GONNA FLOAT
NOW YOU DON'T NEED A BOAT
CAUSE WE ALL GONNA FLOAT
NOW YOU DON'T NEED A BOAT
CAUSE WE ALL GONNA FLOAT
WHEN I DIP ME IN THE GOLDEN
DIP ME IN THE GOLDEN
DIP ME IN THE GOLDEN (DIP ME!)
DIP ME IN THE GOLDEN
DIP ME IN THE GOLDEN SEA!

(*End number, applause, and Olio of* "Waddy Googan" *goes off as set begins to change and MRS. YEAMONS and COMPANY sing.*)

[MUSIC NO. 28A: DOUBLE DIP]

MRS. YEAMONS.
OH DIP ME IN THE GOLDEN SEA
   COMPANY.
DIP ME IN THE GOLDEN SEA
   MRS. YEAMONS.
DIP ME IN THE GOLDEN
   COMPANY.
DIP ME IN THE GOLDEN
   MRS. YEAMONS.
DIP ME IN THE
   COMPANY.
DIP ME IN THE

MRS. YEAMONS.
DIP ME IN
  COMPANY.
DIP ME IN
  MRS. YEAMONS.
DIP ME
  COMPANY.
DIP ME
  MRS. YEAMONS.
DIP DIP DIP DIP DIP DIP DIP DIP
  COMPANY.
DIP DIP DIP DIP DIP DIP DIP DIP
  ALL.
DIP ME!
BATHE ME!
BRETHREN, YOU AND ME!
(*as they start off*)
NOW YOU DON'T NEED A BOAT
CAUSE WE ALL GONNA FLOAT
NOW YOU DON'T NEED A BOAT
CAUSE WE ALL GONNA FLOAT
NOW YOU DON'T NEED A BOAT
CAUSE WE ALL GONNA FLOAT . . .

(*By now all are off save HARRIGAN who crosses to dressing table D.R. as MARTIN HANLEY comes on.*)

HANLEY. Here it is, Ned. Though what you want with it is beyond me.

ANNIE HARRIGAN. (*Coming on as NED takes list from HANLEY*) What is it, dear?

HARRIGAN. A manifest. Third class passengers on that White Star liner that came in yesterday. Listen to these names — Dubrovsky, Goldstein, Polawitz.

HANLEY. More immigrants.

HARRIGAN. With a difference, listen! (*reading*) Kozinko, Lubenkoff, Mankowitz, Petrovsky.

HANLEY. Russians, Poles, and Jews, so what?

HARRIGAN. No Irish that's what! Not a Reilly on board! There's a whole new part of Europe pouring into this country crying to be put on the stage.

HANLEY. Ned, we've done pretty well with the Irish and Germans all these years, that's what the audiences come to see.

HARRIGAN. Today! But tomorrow they'll want what's new and what's new is this! Face it, Martin, the Irish have become respectable.

ANNIE HARRIGAN. God preserve us, it's the end of the race.

HANLEY. But what do you know about Italians, Jews, and Poles?

HARRIGAN. All I have to know is where they are — on the bottom! And while they're working their way up, I write about 'em! (*growing more and more excited*) No more Mulligan Alley, I'll move the plays uptown. Hester Street! And Mulberry! I can be a horsecar conductor — that'll let me go from place to place. Annie can be my wife and Tony. . . . (*He stops. In his enthusiasm he has forgotten. When he speaks again all the excitement has gone out of his voice.*) I forgot. I always forget. Sorry, Martin.

ANNIE HARRIGAN. (*softly*) It's not impossible, you know.

HARRIGAN. What do you mean?

ANNIE HARRIGAN. Tony coming back. That play of his. "Buttons." It's not very good.

HARRIGAN. Who told you this?

HANLEY. Sam Nichols bumped into Fred Wallace. He's booking the tour. He says it'll close in a month.

HARRIGAN. Then there's no hope, Martin. There's only one way Tony could ever come back. On top.

ANNIE HARRIGAN. Maybe not. Tony has his own money in the show and if he loses it he won't be able to go on. And even if he doesn't realize it, Gerta does.

HARRIGAN. You've talked to her?

ANNIE HARRIGAN. She asked me to lunch last week. She's frightened, Ned. Tony's changed, he's not himself. She wants to come back.

HARRIGAN. But has anybody talked to Tony?

HANLEY. (*as LIGHTS start down on ANNIE, himself*) Let Gerta handle it. She talked him into leaving, she can talk him into coming back.

ANNIE HARRIGAN. Give it a few weeks. Wait and see.

[MUSIC NO. 29: THAT'S MY PARTNER REPRISE]

HARRIGAN. (*As MUSIC comes softly up, LIGHTS now almost out on OTHERS.*) All right. We'll give it as many weeks as you want. I'll write Tony's parts for him and as you say, we'll wait and see. (*HARRIGAN, alone in LIGHT, as he sings.*) HE'S MY BROTHER

MY OTHER SELF
I'LL WALK MY DAILY MILE WITH
SMILE WITH COME WHAT MAY
I'M HONORED TO SAY . . .

HE'LL BE BY MY SIDE
FOR LIFETIMES TO COME
MY PARTNER
MY PAL . . .
(*as LIGHTS iris out on HARRIGAN*)
MY CHUM.

[MUSIC NO. 30: I'VE COME HOME TO STAY]

(*And we come up on. . . .*)

SCENE 3

Bare stage of theatre. *One or two flats, pieces of furniture, etc.*
TONY HART, dressed as English swell, singing to piano
accompaniment.

TONY HART.
I'VE NOTHING BUT MONEY AND TIME
TWAS LEFT TO ME BY DEAR OLD DAD
I'VE SPENT EV'RYTHING, ON OH SUCH A FLING
AND WHAT A GOOD TIME I HAVE HAD
THEY CALL ME A REGULAR SWELL . . .
(*He stops for a moment, then continues*)
QUITE ENGLISH WHEREVER I GO
THIS ACCENT I GOT REMARKABLE WELL . . .
(*He hesitates again.*)
    WILLIAM GILL. (*who is watching*) While over in London.
    TONY HART. I know. (*He sings.*)
WHILE OVER IN LONDON, YOU KNOW

OH BUT I'VE COME HOME TO STAY
TO PR-PROMENADE BROADWAY
CROWDS ADORING, GIRLS IMPLORING
D-DON'T YOU GO AWAY
OH WITH . . .
(*He is having difficulty.*)

OH WITH . . .

WILLIAM GILL. Oh with London I'm blasé.

TONY HART. (*angrily*) I know the lyric, I'm just tired. I've been rehearsing all day.

GERTA. (*who has been watching from sidelines*) Of course you are, darling. (*to GILL*) I think that will be enough for today, Mr. Gill.

WILLIAM GILL. May I remind you, Mrs. Hart, that we open in three days!

GERTA. (*as TONY sits in chair, his head in his hands*) I'm aware of that, Mr. Gill, but Mr. Hart is exhausted and there's nothing to be gained by insisting.

WILLIAM GILL. Perhaps we should postpone the opening. It would mean giving up the week in Baltimore but. . . .

GERTA. That won't be necessary, Mr. Gill. As I told you, Mr. Hart is just a bit tired, he'll be fine by tomorrow.

WILLIAM GILL. That's what you said yesterday, Mrs. Hart. I have a reputation to maintain and. . . .

GERTA. I think you'll agree, Mr. Gill, that Mr. Hart has something of a name to uphold too! And if you want my opinion, the best thing you can do for your reputation is to work on some of those endless scenes in Act II. Mr. Hart is an actor, not a magician. (*before he can interrupt*) Now if you don't mind, Mr. Gill, Mr. Hart needs his rest. I'm sure we can continue this conversation another time.

WILLIAM GILL. Now see here, Mrs. Hart. . . .

GERTA. Goodnight, Mr. Gill! (*She turns from him, starts* U.S. *to where she has left her coat. He stands there for a moment, then angrily starts out* R. *GERTA takes her coat, starts to TONY.*) Tony. (*no answer*) It's after six, Tony. I told the cab to be waiting from five-thirty. (*He stirs, still doesn't answer.*) The company's gone, Tony. I'm sure they want to lock up.

TONY HART. (*his voice a bit hoarse*) You go on. Don't keep the cab waiting.

GERTA. And what will you do?

TONY HART. I want to stay here a few more minutes.

GERTA. I counted on your coming home with me tonight, Tony. There's something we have to discuss.

TONY HART. When am I going to learn Act II?

GERTA. That's part of it. But not the important part.

TONY HART. What is the important part, Gerta?

GERTA. I'd rather not discuss it here, Tony, it's far too serious.

TONY HART. Don't play games, Gerta. And don't waste your time. I won't be home tonight so out with it now or it'll have to keep.

GERTA. Really, Tony, I'm not accustomed to being talked to in this. . . .

TONY HART. Don't waste your time, Gerta!

GERTA. All right, Tony, it's the play. (*turning to him*) It isn't any good.

TONY HART. Is that all?

GERTA. All? It's everything! Don't you understand — the play's bad! It won't work!

TONY HART. Old news, Gerta. I've known how bad it was for months. So if that's all. . . .

GERTA. It's not all! I think we ought to close it and go back. Yes, to Harrigan. (*a rush of words*) I had lunch with Annie the other day. And I told her we might be willing to — to discuss things.

TONY HART. Did you now?

GERTA. I did it for you, Tony! I could see how unhappy you were. These headaches, not being able to learn your lines, losing your voice — it's all because you don't like the play. So I decided to put my interests aside and. . . .

TONY HART. By "your interests," Gerta, do you mean *you* want to continue with "Buttons"?

GERTA. Well I am playing a starring part and. . . .

TONY HART. Then I couldn't let you sacrifice yourself, Gerta. Your interests are my interests. I couldn't think of dropping the play.

GERTA. I'm trying to explain, Tony, that I am putting aside my interests for the greater good! And if you're concerned about Ned's reaction I can assure you he'll welcome you with open arms.

TONY HART. All I have to do is say Ned I'm sorry, please take me back, is that it?

GERTA. Just say anything. I'm sure he'll be only too willing to forgive and forget.

TONY HART. Can I believe my ears? Are you talking about the same Ned Harrigan you said was using me all these years? You'd better run along, Gerta. Your cab's waiting.

GERTA. Tony, this is serious! We must go back!

TONY HART. No, Gerta, that is *not* what we must do. What we must do is open the play. And tour it till it dies a nice natural death. After all, you've got a starring part and you've already sacrificed enough for me. For your sake, dear, we mustn't give up.

GERTA. All right, Tony, if you want me to say it I will! The play is awful and we're going to be awful in it! And it's taking every cent we have to put it on so won't you please listen to reason.

TONY HART. Lies, Gerta. Sweet little wifely lies. And all for me, I'm touched. But I won't let you do it, darling. This time we're going to think of you. A real man always thinks of his wife first.

GERTA. Tony, I. . . .

TONY HART. (*overriding her, seizing her by shoulders, harshly*) We're doing the play! Till it finishes or we do! (*before she can speak*) I don't turn back, Gerta, is that clear? (*seizing her by the wrist*) I said, *Is that clear?*

GERTA. (*After a moment, softly, the fight is out of her.*) Yes, Tony.

TONY HART. Now go on home, I have an appointment.

GERTA. Business?

TONY HART. Business.

GERTA. (*as she starts out*) Don't stay out too late, Tony, we have a rehearsal at ten tomorrow and. . . .

TONY HART. Goodnight, Gerta.

GERTA. Goodnight.

(*And she goes. TONY is alone.*)

[MUSIC NO. 31: IF I COULD TRUST ME]

(*MUSIC comes softly up as he looks out at the empty house, then sings.*)

TONY.
IF I COULD TRUST ME I'D BEGIN
LIVING WITHOUT
HIDING WITHIN
IF I COULD TRUST ME

IF I COULD REACH THE MAN INSIDE
BANISH HIS FEARS

WAKEN HIS PRIDE
IF I COULD TRUST ME
THEN WITH THE COURAGE TO SPEAK FROM MY
   HEART
I'D FOLLOW ITS WILL
UNTIL I START

MAKING THE BOY WHO HIDES WITHIN
INTO THE MAN
HE MIGHT HAVE BEEN
THE MAN HE WAS MEANT TO BE
IF I COULD JUST TRUST ME!

(*The MUSIC of* "Wonderful Me" *comes quietly up through
   this. TONY listens, remembering, then softly sings the last
   line:*)

—CAUSE AFTER ALL IS SAID AND DONE
YOU'LL FIND THAT EV'RY SINGLE WONDERFUL ONE
   OF THEM'S
WONDERFUL ME!

(*Somehow, remembering what he felt at that time gives him new
   courage, and it is with a desperate kind of hope that he
   continues:*)

THEN WITH THE COURAGE TO LEAD WITH MY
   HEART
I'D FOLLOW ITS WILL
UNTIL I START

MAKING THE BOY WHO HIDES WITHIN
INTO THE MAN
HE MIGHT HAVE BEEN
THE MAN HE WAS MEANT TO BE . . .
(*as he starts slowly off*)
IF I COULD JUST
TRUST
ME.

(*MUSIC fades, LIGHTS fade, as we come up on . . .*)

Scene 4

NED HARRIGAN at breakfast table. ANNIE HARRIGAN with him. NED has just crumpled a newspaper he was reading.)

HARRIGAN. It's filthy! They shouldn't be allowed to print things like that. This paper, the Graphic, it's never to be brought in this house again.

ANNIE HARRIGAN. I'm sorry, Ned. I thought you'd want to know.

HARRIGAN. Well, I don't! Why can't they leave Tony alone.

ANNIE HARRIGAN. But if it's true?

HARRIGAN. It isn't true! I know Tony as well as I know myself. It's a lie. A filthy insinuation. I don't want to hear another word about it.

ANNIE HARRIGAN. But. . . .

HARRIGAN. Annie, no more. It isn't true. That's all.

(And up on DOCTOR's Office. *GERTA is waiting as DOCTOR comes in.)*

DOCTOR. Sorry to keep you waiting, Mrs. Hart. It took nearly a half-hour to get back from 14th Street. The traffic in this city is . . . .

GERTA. (*as we become aware of her growing tension and nervousness through this scene*) I don't mean to interrupt you, Doctor, but Mr. Hart is waiting for me. We have a rehearsal this afternoon.

DOCTOR. Of course, I understand, a new play already? How did the other one do—"The Maid and The Moonshiner"?

GERTA. Not too well, I'm afraid. But I didn't realize we were here to discuss the theatrical season, Doctor.

DOCTOR. I'm sorry. It's just that this is rather difficult to say and that's why I asked to see you alone. I'm afraid I've bad news for you, Mrs. Hart. Of course you'll want to consult other doctors but from all I could see yesterday Mr. Hart's loss of voice is just a symptom of a more serious disturbance.

GERTA. I hope you're not going to repeat that filth in the Graphic! Mr. Hart is in perfect health. He feels as well as ever.

DOCTOR. He may feel well, Mrs. Hart, but I assure you he isn't. Of course, with further examination, a few weeks in a private clinic. . . .

GERTA. What are you talking about? He's in rehearsal for a new play! There's a tour all booked! Oh, I know how these things work. Another patient coming in with the same complaint would get a few pills and be sent home, but because Mr. Hart is a celebrity it's further examinations and private clinics! I think it's disgusting!

DOCTOR. Very well, Mrs. Hart, if you feel that way I suggest you see someone else. Doctor Avery—or Engel at the New York Hospital. Both are expert blood men. . . .

GERTA. I'll see them both, Doctor. *After* the play opens! By which time Mr. Hart's symptoms will probably have completely disappeared. You can send us your bill whenever you wish. Good day, Doctor.

DOCTOR. Good day, Mrs. Hart. (*looking after her as she goes*) Good day.

[MUSIC NO. 32: UNDERSCORE—MAGGIE REPRISE]

(*A* Dressing Room L. *ANNIE YEAMONS and ADA LEWIS putting on makeup as MARTIN HANLEY and LILY FAY rehearse softly* U.R.)

MRS. YEAMONS. I couldn't go backstage! What could I say?

ADA LEWIS. Did Tony know you were there?

MRS. YEAMONS. I suppose so, but what could I do? It's not the play, it's Tony! He dropped lines, stuttered, forgot his cues. I couldn't stay.

ADA LEWIS. Have you told Ned?

MRS. YEAMONS. He's up to his neck getting ready for the tour, what good would it do? Anyhow I spoke to Gerta, she says Tony won't see him—Oh my God, it's our cue!

HANLEY AND LILY.
ON SUNDAY NIGHT
'TIS MY DELIGHT
AND PLEASURE
DON'T YOU SEE

TO MEET ALL THE GIRLS
AND ALL THE BOYS
WHO WORK DOWNTOWN
WITH ME

THERE'S AN ORGAN
IN THE PARLOR
TO GIVE THE HOUSE
A TONE . . .

MRS. YEAMONS AND ADA LEWIS. (*hastily sticking their heads out on stage*)
AND YOU ARE WELCOME ANY EVENING!
ALL FOUR.
AT MAGGIE MURPHY'S HOME.
MRS. YEAMONS. (*as they sit back down*) Poor Tony.
ADA LEWIS. Poor kid.

(*Up on* Stage of Theatre, *TONY HART, dressed as Old Irish-woman, in middle of rehearsal. His voice is harsh, hoarse.*)

TONY HART. And a fig for your claims, Captain! The property's mine and stays mine and no upstart of an Ulsterman says d. . . . diff. . . . (*He has a hard time with the word.*) Different. Now all of ye. . . . gath. . . . gather round and. . . . (*The line is gone.*) Gather round and. . . . Give me that cue, dammit!
OFFSTAGE VOICE. Gather round and we'll have a. . . .
TONY HART. We'll have a celebration! A. . . . a celebration.
GILL'S VOICE. We'll have a celebration to. . . .
TONY HART. I know it! A celebration to. . . . We'll have a celebration. . . . (*as scene fades*) A celebration. A. . . .

(*MARTIN HANLEY and HARRY MACK on the street*)

[MUSIC NO. 32A: AFTER MAGGIE REPRISE]

HANLEY. (*reading from tabloid*) Here it is again. The third article this month. "That Tell-Tale Stutter. Is Tony Hart The Victim Of An Unmentionable Blood Disease?"
HARRY MACK. I saw it. Anyway, I knew. Engel at New York Hospital is a friend of the family. Tony went to see him last week.
HANLEY. Then it's true.
HARRY MACK. There's no hope, Martin, the disease is in its last stages. An institution would be the best place for him but Gerta refuses. They need the money and Tony's got that new play.
HANLEY. He can't do a show! Not like this.
HARRY MACK. Not for long anyway. The stuttering is just a beginning. His voice will go, his sense of balance, his memory. . .
HANLEY. Ned won't go on tour when he hears this.
HARRY MACK. (*As MUSIC is heard in distance, LIGHTS*

start going down on HANLEY and MACK.) What good would it do him to stay? He's been down to Tony's theatre twice this week. [MUSIC NO. 33: I'VE COME HOME TO STAY REPRISE] (*as they exit*) The doorman gave him the message. Mr. Hart was out.

(*And up on* Stage of Theatre *where TONY's show is in performance. TONY seems his old self as with FOUR GIRLS behind him he sings:*)

TONY HART.
OH BUT I'VE COME HOME TO STAY
TO PROMENADE BROADWAY
CROWDS ADORING, GIRLS IMPLORING
DON'T YOU GO AWAY . . .
(*A hesitation, then*)
OH WITH LONDON I'M BLASÉ
IT'S FOG BOTH NIGHT AND DAY
(*He stops. Panic is written on his face. He repeats the line.*)
IT'S FOG BOTH NIGHT AND DAY . . .
(*again*)
IT'S FOG . . . It's fog. . . .
(*We can hear the harsh rasp of his breathing as he finally gasps.*)
Ned. (*then louder*) Ned, Ned. . . . (*a shout*)
NED!!

(*And immediately up on. . . .*)

SCENE 5

A Hospital Corridor, *late afternoon, the sun streaming through some high rectangular window somewhere. Faintly from outside the sounds of children playing, street music. GERTA sitting on bench, NAT GOODWIN beside her.*

NAT GOODWIN. Not one seat left in the entire theatre! It was sold out twenty-four hours after we announced it. Nearly fourteen thousand dollars, that's the most money ever collected at a benefit performance since they started the damn things. Enough to pay all the bills and take care of Tony as long as. . . . (*not able to look at her*) As long as he lives.
GERTA. Thank you, Nat. We both appreciate it.

NAT GOODWIN. I only hope he'll be well enough to come, every star in town's going to be on that stage.

GERTA. Ned too?

NAT GOODWIN. I didn't ask him, Gerta. He's out on tour and. . . .

GERTA. I want him asked, Nat. I'll wire him this afternoon.

NAT GOODWIN. Let me do it for you, Gerta, it'll be easier.

GERTA. No, Nat, I want it to come from me. I suppose it's a bit late to say I'm sorry, but it's the only chance I'll have.

NURSE. (*coming on from left*) He's awake now, Mrs. Hart.

GERTA. I'll be right there, Nurse. (*to NAT*) I'd ask you in but he doesn't always remember people and it upsets him. And don't tell anyone about Ned coming. In case he refuses. [MUSIC NO. 34: I NEED THIS ONE CHANCE] I couldn't blame him, you know. (*putting out her hand*) Goodbye, Nat. And thank you. (*NAT GOODWIN leaves, GERTA is alone, as she sings:*)

I NEED THIS ONE CHANCE
TO SAY I WAS WRONG
TO TELL HIM HOW BLIND
I'VE BEEN ALL ALONG
TO THE BOY, TO THE MAN, TO THE DREAM

ONE CHANCE TO HOLD HIM
AND TRY TO ERASE
THE ANGER AND HURT
I SEE IN HIS FACE
AND TO TELL HIM I'M NOT WHAT I SEEM

I DON'T WANT TO MAKE EXCUSES
I'M TIRED OF PRETENDING I KNOW ALL THE ANSWERS
AND IT'S NOT THAT I WANT FORGIVENESS
I DON'T NEED THEIR PARDON TO LIVE!

I NEED THIS ONE CHANCE
TO SAY I WAS WRONG
SO MAYBE SOME DAY
SOMEHOW
SOME WAY
I CAN FORGIVE . . .
MYSELF.

(*End song, LIGHTS fade, GERTA starts off as we come up on*

MARTIN HANLEY as ANNIE HARRIGAN hurries on from L.) [MUSIC NO. 34A: AFTER ONE CHANCE]

[MUSIC NO. 35: FOLLOW A BAND REPRISE]

ANNIE HARRIGAN. (*And through this music of* "Follow The Band" *is heard in background and set begins to change from* Hospital Corridor *to* Academy of Music.) He's agreed! We close here Saturday, put the company on a train, and get to New York Sunday morning.

HANLEY. I'll wire Nat right away.

ANNIE HARRIGAN. Tell him we'll be doing a few of the old songs, then Ned'll do Mulligan Guards with Annie Yeamons. (*HANLEY stops.*) I know, Martin, but Gerta asked for it. (*as they start* U.S. *to join COMPANY who have begun to assemble*) Just one chorus. Right after the opening. . . .

(*Through last of this HARRIGAN and NAT GOODWIN come on* L. *as ANNIE and MARTIN HANLEY join COMPANY as they begin verse of number.*)

NAT. Tony won't be here, Ned. Gerta spoke to the doctors but they won't let him leave the hospital. She hopes you'll understand

HARRIGAN. Of course, Nat, of course. (*stopping*) Nat. Tony's not coming, it isn't because of me, is it?

NAT. I wish I could say it was, Ned. He's too sick to leave his room. (*gently*) You've got to get into costume, Ned. Annie's on.

HARRIGAN. All right, Nat. I'm coming.

ANNIE/HANLEY/COMPANY.
MUSIC CHARMED THE DEACON
A MEMBER OF THE CHURCH
HE'D HEAR A BAND AND WEAKEN
IT CHARMED HIM OFF HIS PERCH

ONE DAY WITH THE COLLECTION
BEHIND THE BAND HE FLED
AND WHEN THEY CAUGHT HIM
LATE THAT NIGHT
WHY THIS IS WHAT HE SAID . . .

(*By this time ANNIE/HANLEY, and COMPANY have swung around full front and we find ourselves on the. . . .*)

SCENE 6

Stage of the Academy of Music *the night of the benefit as AN-NIE and full COMPANY, save for HARRIGAN and MRS. YEAMONS, sing.*

ANNIE AND COMPANY.
TARA, TARA TARA, I HEARD THEM CORNETS PLAY
BIM BUM, THEY BEAT THE DRUM, MY FEET BEGAN
   TO SWAY
SOUSA, I DO DECLARE, YOUR MARCHES AM SO GRAND
JUST CAN'T STOP, AWAY I HOP
I LOVE TO FOLLOW A BAND
(*Short Dance section, then ALL sing.*)
JUST CAN'T STOP, AWAY I HOP
I LOVE TO FOLLOW A BAND!

(*Number ends as MUSIC seques to a more gentle strain and Olio goes up to reveal the old Mulligan Alley drop. MRS. YEA-MONS comes strolling down through the COMPANY as HARRIGAN, in Mulligan Guard costume, enters from L.*)

MRS. YEAMONS. (*as MUSIC softly continues*) Well, upon my soul, if it isn't old Mulligan! What are you doing back in the old neighborhood?

HARRIGAN. (*This isn't easy for him.*) Oh, just out for a stroll. I was thinking about Mulligan Alley and I wondered if the old street had changed. It has, Annie.

MRS. YEAMONS. Not that much, dear. Some of the folks used to live here is gone, but the old block's the same. Oh what times we had here then, Mulligan! Remember the fights, and the dancing, and the shouting, and the noise.

HARRIGAN. I'll never forget it, Annie. Never. (*The MUSIC fades.*)

MRS. YEAMONS. And that funny old song we used to sing. Nobody knows the words any more, I guess, but I liked it. (*She is near tears.*) Now how did it go again? [MUSIC NO. 36: MULLIGAN

REPRISE] (*The familiar MUSIC comes softly up.*) Oh yes. (*And
ad-lib she sings.*)
WE CRAVE YOUR CONDESCENSION
TO TELL YOU WHAT WE KNOW
  HARRIGAN.
OF MARCHING IN THE MULLIGAN GUARD
FROM BAXTER STREET BELOW
  MRS. YEAMONS AND HARRIGAN.
OUR CAPTAIN'S NAME WAS HUSSEY
A TIPPERARY MAN
HE CARRIED HIS SWORD LIKE A RUSSIAN DUKE
WHENEVER HE TOOK COMMAND . . .

(*They are about to continue, when a VOICE from* U.L. *suddenly sings the next line.*)

  VOICE. (*softly*)
WE SHOULDERED ARMS
AND MARCHED AND MARCHED AWAY . . .
(*Through this stage begins to clear and we see TONY HART,
wearing his old costume, singing his old lines. ANNIE
YEAMONS turns to him as the OTHERS go softly off. HAR-
RIGAN does not move as TONY, with effort, continues.*)
FROM BAXTER STREET
WE MARCHED TO AVENUE A
THE . . . THE DRUMS . . .
  HARRIGAN. (*By now stage is almost cleared, MRS. YEA-
MONS has started off.*)
AND FIFES, HOW SWEETLY THEY DID PLAY!

(*NED has turned to him as TONY starts slowly to him.*)

  BOTH.
AS WE MARCHED, MARCHED, MARCHED
IN THE MULLIGAN GUARD!

(*NED has put his arm around TONY's shoulder and they begin
the Dance. TONY falters once, but with NED's strength
alongside him he gets through. As LIGHTS begin to change,
so do NED and TONY. They grow stronger, younger, the
Academy of Music disappears, with the Mulligan Alley*

*drop, and as the MUSIC gets louder, and clearer, the BOYS
become as they were that wonderful day at the Comique all
those years ago as bathed in LIGHT on a bare glowing stage
they sing.*)

HARRIGAN AND HART.
WHEN THE BAND PLAYED GARRY OWEN
OR THE CONNAMARA PET
WITH A RUB DUB DUB, WE'D MARCH IN THE MUD
TO A MILITARY STEP
WITH THE GREEN ABOVE THE RED, BOYS
TO SHOW WHERE WE COME FROM
OUR GUNS WE'D LIFT WITH A RIGHT SHOULDER
    SHIFT
AS WE MARCHED TO THE BEAT OF THE DRUM
(*They shine with joy, youth, and excitement.*)
WE SHOULDERED ARMS
AND MARCHED AND MARCHED AWAY
FROM BAXTER STREET
WE MARCHED TO AVENUE A
WITH DRUMS AND FIFES
HOW SWEETLY THEY DID PLAY
AS WE MARCHED, MARCHED, MARCHED
IN THE MULLIGAN GUARD . . .
(*dance*)
AS WE MARCHED, MARCHED, MARCHED
IN THE MULLIGAN
MARCHED, MARCHED, MARCHED
IN THE MULLIGAN . . .
MARCHED, MARCHED, MARCHED
IN THE MULLIGAN GUARD . . .

(*NED and TONY, as they were that first opening night,* the
    same staging as when the scene was originally played)

HARRIGAN. Do you hear that? They like us!
TONY HART. And why shouldn't they? We're wonderful!
HARRIGAN. And this is only the beginning, Tony! We'll get a
company, build a theatre, write plays with music to sing to,
march to, dance to, music all over 'em!
TONY HART. (*Laughing, as he starts after him.*) Wait for me,
Neddy! Wait for me!

(*A freeze for NED and TONY. NED reaching out, TONY*

reaching after him, as one by one, the COMPANY starts on and sings.)

[MUSIC NO. 37: FINALE — SOMETHING NEW]

COMPANY.
SOMETHING NEW!
SOMETHING DIFF'RENT!
SOMETHING NEVER SEEN BEFORE
SOMETHING UNEXPLORED AND FRESH AS EARLY
  SPRING . . .
(Through following, freeze comes to life, NED puts his arm around TONY's shoulder and both men start slowly off L.)
SOMETHING NEW
SOMETHING DIFF'RENT
SOMETHING NEVER EVEN TRIED
SOMETHING LOOKING LIKE IT'S DONE AS IF BY
  CHANCE . . .

WE'LL SING!
WE'LL DANCE!

SOMETHING NEW
SOMETHING DIFF'RENT
SOMETHING WAITING IN THE WINGS
SOMETHING SET TO MAKE AN ENTRANCE — TAKE
  A BOW
WHEN WE COME SAILING THROUGH THE DOOR
WITH SOMETHING NEW AND FURTHERMORE
SOMETHING NEVER DONE BEFORE . . .
(By now NED and TONY have added hats to their Mulligan Guards costumes, come out R. and L., join C. to stand with TONY leaning on NED's shoulder, as COMPANY sings:)
TILL NOW!!

(BLACKOUT, and that is. . . .)

THE END OF THE SHOW

[MUSIC NO. 38: BOWS #1]
[MUSIC NO. 38A: FINAL BOWS]
[MUSIC NO. 39: EXIT MUSIC]